Racing Away With His Heart

CJ Bower

Acknowledgements:

I have an amazing team behind me that I would never have been able to make it this far without. To the La Crosse Area Writers Group, thank you for being my personal hack-and-maim squad.

My beta readers, who became just as invested in my characters as I have. And to a wonderful circle of friends, for always believing in me, even if I don't always believe in myself. I couldn't have done this, or gotten as far in my writing career, without any of you. My deepest and most heart-felt, gratitude.

And most importantly, my readers. I appreciate every one of you, and I thank you for joining me on this incredible journey.

Dedication:

Thank you, Dad, for getting me addicted to horsepower, the smells of exhaust fumes and burning rubber, and the adrenaline rush that is auto racing.

Chapter 1

The private jet touched down smoothly at the Charlotte-Douglas International Airport Thursday morning, the late-May sunshine bathing the cabin's interior. Nisa covered her stomach with her hand, trying to calm the dancing butterflies as the plane rolled to the executive hangar.

"Wow," Emmie descended the steps to the tarmac and to the waiting limo. "Talk about the lap of luxury."

"Having a professional athlete for a brother has its perks." Nisa shrugged, following her best friend. "But life wasn't as extravagant when Daddy raced."

"I didn't know that," Emmie said.

The steward passed their luggage to the waiting chauffeur, who stowed the bags into the trunk of the long, pearl-gray limo and snapped the lid closed, then opened the rear door.

"Thank you." Nisa slid into the cool, dark interior, the sumptuous brown leather enveloping her in comfort and extravagance. Wow. Her brother had done well for himself in NASCAR's top level.

The chauffeur touched his fingers to the brim of his cap as Emmie joined Nisa inside. "Ma'am."

He closed the door and slid behind the wheel. Nisa raised the privacy shield between front and back.

"How charming." Emmie's voice was saccharine sweet.

"Shut up." Nisa giggled as the limo started rolling. "Anyway, the sport has changed so much in twenty years. Daddy was lucky to make as much in half a season then as Cole can in one race now."

"So, where are we staying?" Emmie asked as the limo turned onto the beltway bypassing downtown near the Panthers' football stadium, which was visible from the right-side window. "Charlotte is *huge*!"

"Yeah, it is," Nisa agreed, looking out at the skyscrapers towering over the city streets. "I hated it when we moved here from Darlington. But Daddy's career was reaching its peak and Cole's was just starting to take off." She twined her fingers, picking a hangnail along her left thumb. "I *still* hate it."

"Because of your dad?"

Nisa looked at her friend. "Probably." She faced the window again as she remembered the conversation that convinced her to board the plane. "Mr. Kincade wanted to put us up in a hotel suite downtown, but I called Cole and asked if we could use his motor coach instead."

Vincent Kincade, the general manager of the Charlotte Motor Speedway, had called her a few months ago, asking her to come to Charlotte for the memorial commemorating the 20th anniversary of her father's death.

She'd balked, but gentle prodding from her brother had changed her mind. He'd said it was important to him for her to be there, so she'd reluctantly called Vincent back to confirm her attendance.

The rest of the drive was calmer. But as soon as the limo drove through the tunnel under the track, sweat dotted Nisa's brow and her lungs tightened as the car inched closer to their destination. When they rolled to a stop at the security station, Nisa signed for their credentials with trembling fingers.

"Are you all right?" Emmie rubbed Nisa's back lightly.

Nisa took a deep breath, trying to slow her racing heart as they climbed back into the limo with their hot passes, which granted them access to the restricted areas of the infield. "I – I don't know if I can do this."

"Do what?" Emmie frowned as she took the lanyard from Nisa.

"This," she said, gesturing to encompass the whole track.

"Be here?" Emmie asked, hugging her. "It'll be fine. You'll be surrounded by family."

What's left of it. Nisa pointed toward the turn three wall as the limo headed for the private RV lot. "I still don't know how Cole can come back here year after year, passing that same spot lap after lap."

"Oh. Where your dad …"

Nisa nodded, choking back a sob.

"Do you need anything?" Emmie asked. "Water? Vodka? Maybe some Xanax?"

Nisa chuckled in spite of – or maybe because of – her nerves. "All three?"

Emmie grinned. "That's my girl."

The driver helped both ladies out before seeing to the luggage in the trunk. Nisa passed the man a tip, and he touched a finger to the brim of his cap again as Cole stepped from the coach. With his dark hair, bottle-green eyes and athletic good looks, her brother was a spitting image of their father.

"Thank you," Cole said to the driver, then lifted the luggage into his motor coach.

Nisa recognized the Zephyr right away, and knew the nondescript exterior belied the deluxe accommodations inside. She followed Emmie up the steps as Cole set the suitcases in the sitting area. "Nice upgrades, big brother."

Cole grinned. "I think so, too."

They were both thinking of the ramshackle fifth-wheel he'd called home for the first five years of his racing career. Nisa looked around. Four flat-screen televisions were fixed at various points around the interior. A glassed-in cabinet was built behind the cockpit seats, where Cole kept the Blu-ray player and a vast movie collection. Sumptuous, butter-soft emerald green leather covered the sofas flanking either side of the center aisle, and the soft recessed lighting in the ceiling lent a cozy, relaxing atmosphere.

"You can stay in my room," Cole said to Nisa.

"Wait. I'm sleeping on the couch?" Emmie squealed.

"It pulls out into a bed." Cole touched a button on the wall panel, and the bed emerged from the belly of the sofa. "I've taken plenty of naps on it. You'll be fine."

Emmie sat on the mattress, testing the comfort. "I guess it'll do," she said at last.

"Let me show you where you can sleep." He picked up Nisa's suitcase and headed for the rear of the coach. "Dang, sis! What did you pack? The kitchen sink?"

"No," she scoffed. "Everything but."

Cole chuckled, setting the case on the floor in the bedroom. His expression sobered as he turned to her, wrapping her in a hug. "How are you feeling?"

"I'm fine," she said with false brightness.

Cole pulled back and studied her with an intensity that made her nerves jump even more.
"You're not fine, Nisa. You're really pale." He sighed. "Is it from being at the track?"

She gave up the pretense, her shoulders sagging. "I – I don't know how you can do it."

Cole shrugged. "I can't think about it."

"How can you *not*?" she wailed. "It's all I can think about. Daddy was *killed* at this track, Cole!"

"I know, Nisa." His voice was quiet, calm. "I was here when it happened."

"And yet you still race." Her tone was sharper than she'd intended, and she grimaced.

"Yes, I still race. I race in his memory. His honor, as well as my own," he explained. "Nisa, if you can't stand being here this weekend, I'll tell Mr. Kincade to take you back home. I won't make you stay here if you can't handle it."

"I – I thought I could." Her heart still pounding, she turned away. "But now …"

"Now you're not so sure."

She shook her head. "No, I'm not."

His arms wrapped around her waist. "Is there anything I can do to make it easier?"

"Short of sending me home? Probably not."

"It really means a lot to me that you're here, Nisa."

"I know." The enormity of the situation almost crushed her. She and Cole had always shared a close relationship, and she didn't want to jeopardize that. "I'm scared."

"I know, sis. But you made it this far." He turned her in his arms and kissed her forehead. "You have the courage to face your fear, and maybe find some closure. I'll be right here with you every step of the way."

"Thank you."

"You're welcome." He inclined his head, smiling. "Let's give Emmie the whole VIP experience."

Nisa smiled back. "I'm sure she'd like that."

Chapter 2

Nisa sat in the back of the golf cart behind Cole, her mind lost in her emotions. Still swamped with anxiety, she hadn't said much when her brother had picked her and Emmie up for the party.

"Where are we going?" Emmie asked later as Cole whisked them through the infield on a golf cart.

"The whole weekend is packed with parties and concerts," Cole explained, naming one of the hottest acts currently topping the charts. "I hope you like country music."

Emmie bounced excitedly in her seat, thanking Cole repeatedly for the opportunity. Nisa's own reaction was lackluster, as she was still nervous and she wished she could be as nonchalant about being at the track as Cole was. The music carried from the concert when he dropped them off at the entrance of the open venue. Nisa and Emmie climbed out and waited for him at the gate as the crowd swallowed Cole's cart.

"It's total chaos!" Emmie shouted over the crowd and music. "It'll take him forever!"

Nisa grinned. "No, it won't! Cole said that there's front-row parking for drivers and track officials in case they need to leave in a hurry." She saw him weaving through the throng of people a couple minutes later. "See? There he is now."

Their other friend, Shayna, had been right. Cole was hot. His dark hair was threaded with silver at the temples, giving him a distinguished air. He was only about five-nine, but the way he carried himself made him appear much taller. However, Nisa still couldn't bring herself to think of him being with her best friend. When he came into full view, four barely-dressed women hung on his arms.

If they're hoping for a hookup, they'll be sorely disappointed.

Cole always had the charisma that drew women like bees to honey, but Nisa knew he preferred women who were modest over those who blatantly displayed their assets. He said he preferred to do the chasing, not the other way around. She didn't blame him. Their oldest sibling, Angela, had turned herself into a pit lizard. The lifestyle had literally killed her; she'd contracted a devastating disease and died the year before their father. Nisa watched as he disengaged himself from the half-dressed women with ease as he returned to her side.

"Problems?" she teased.

He grimaced. "Nothing a fire hose can't take care of." He offered Nisa and Emmie each an arm. "Let's go."

Nisa giggled. "Aww. Poor baby. Must be tough being a successful stock car driver."

"Shut up," he warned, but she could tell there was no real heat to the threat.

"I envy you guys," Emmie said from the other side of Cole as they walked to an open table set up in the VIP area. "I wish I was as close to my brother as you guys are."

"It didn't come without a price." Cole helped Emmie into her seat.

Nisa caught her friend's wince, and knew they were both thinking back to when Nisa had confided to Emmie about losing both her parents; her mother at six months old, then her father when she was ten. Nisa had a feeling Cole's aversion to sexually-forward women stemmed from Angela's death.

The three of them enjoyed the music for a few minutes, before Cole stood up again. "Do you guys want a drink?" he shouted in the lull between songs. Emmie requested a piña colada, while Nisa requested flavored water. Cole headed for the bar on the other side of the roped-off area.

"Oh, God. He's gorgeous!" Emmie shouted at Nisa, pointing.

Nisa looked in the direction of Emmie's finger, and gasped.

Walking through the crowd with ease was a man dressed in tight jeans, a Western shirt, and cowboy boots. His hair was partially hidden beneath his baseball cap, but his face was occasionally illuminated by flashes of light from the stage. *Oh, he's handsome!* And the way his lip quirked up at one corner was sexy. His walk was that of a man who was confident in his own body, and aware of his effect on women, but didn't feel the need to swagger.

Nisa suddenly felt the need to fan herself. Mr. Hotness had made eye contact with her, and a slow smile broke out across his face. She nearly melted from the nuclear blast of that grin. And then he was right in front of their table.

"Good evening, ladies." He came to a halt on the other side of the rope. "May I have the next dance?"

Heat seared Nisa when she realized he was asking her. "Oh…um…" she stuttered.

"She'd love to," Emmie accepted for her.

"Em!" Nisa exclaimed, mortified.

The man's eyes danced with mirth as he held his hand out and lifted up the rope for her. "Shall we?"

****

Tyson Patterson had taken one look at the brunette sitting at the table, and knew he had to meet her. Too bad she'd come with his on-track arch nemesis, Cole Forester. Ty wasn't sure what it was about the other driver that rubbed him the wrong way, but he figured their heated rivalry had started at Bristol three years ago, when Ty had lost control of his car and spun, slamming into Cole and sent his car hard into the outside retaining wall. Ty had thought it was an on-track incident at that time, but somehow it got around the infield that he'd done it deliberately. His professional integrity had been called into question that night, which had hurt him more than he'd cared to admit. Cole had been a thorn in his side ever since.

Maybe that was it – Cole seemed above reproach, that he could do nothing wrong – that kept Ty from being amiable with his competitor. He'd lost track of how many times he'd lost by a nose to Cole. It seemed every time he crossed the finish line the last couple seasons, Cole beat him to it.

Ty was tired of playing second-fiddle to the other driver.

Asking the woman to dance was part of his plan to lure her away from his rival, but now he realized that his motives were entirely selfish. Still, he was glad the pretty, curvy woman sitting at the table accepted for her. His heart thumped when she slipped her hand in his as she ducked beneath the security rope.

The well-known country band switched from a fast-beat dance song to a slow ballad. Ty turned her into his arms. Her head tucked perfectly beneath his chin as he swayed in time to the music. He spun her out, brought her back, then twirled her. He looked deep into her eyes. In this light they looked dark, and he suddenly ached to see what color they were. Her hair, where the ends brushed against his hands as they danced, felt like the finest silk against his skin. He wanted to see it fanned beneath her against his sheets.

"What's your name, darlin'?" he drawled.

"Ni – Nisa." She smiled. "Yours?"

Her voice had a smoky quality that set him on fire. "Ty. How are you likin' the party so far?"

She cocked her head to the side as emotion clouded her vision. "It's weird being back here," she said.

Her answer intrigued him. "Here? Or in Charlotte?"

"Either. Both." She shrugged as best she could in his embrace. "It's my first time back in twenty years."

She didn't look older than twenty-seven or twenty-eight. "Why did you move away?" he asked.

"Personal reasons," she said.

Her evasive response piqued his curiosity even more. After twirling her around again he pressed for more. "What kind of personal reasons?"

"You really know how to dance," she commented, avoiding his question.

His face heated from embarrassment. "My mama was a professional ballroom dancer. She taught my brother and me."

"Do you dance professionally, too?" Nisa asked.

"No, I'm afraid I don't." Ty chuckled. "My brother got that skill."

"Could've fooled me."

The words were mumbled beneath her breath, but, despite the loud music, he heard them anyway. He responded by spinning her out, then bringing her back and sliding her into a suggestive dip with his thigh wedged between hers.

"You're a natural, darlin'," he said, before righting her again. Her blush was endearing as he tucked her beneath his chin. In his line of work he hadn't met very many women who could still do that.

When the song ended, Ty was reluctant to take her back to the table, because he knew Cole would be waiting.

He reluctantly led her back toward the roped-off VIP area, though he stepped back before Cole could spot him.

"What are you doin' for lunch tomorrow?" he asked.

She shrugged. "I – I'm not sure."

He took her hand in his and rubbed his thumb over her knuckles. Her pulse skittered beneath his touch. He loved that she couldn't hide her reaction. "I want to see you again, Nisa. Please meet me for lunch."

"I – we'll see."

It wasn't an outright no, so he'd take what he could get. "Well, if you make up your mind, I'll be at the Speedway Club at eleven-thirty."

Ty couldn't resist the temptation any longer. He cupped her cheek, his thumb stroking along her jaw. The satin skin beneath his touch went to his head faster than the single-malt scotch his father favored. Ty tilted her face up to his, and he inhaled her sweet fragrance as their lips met in a kiss that rocked his very foundations. He pulled back, frowning. He hadn't expected such an explosion from one simple caress. If the dazed look in her eyes was anything to go by, she was just as stunned.

Somehow it didn't help him feel better about it. "I'd better get you back to your friends."

****

Nisa blinked a few times to clear her vision as Ty practically frog-marched her back to the table. The sudden anger in his voice threw her off-guard.

"Did I do something wrong?" she asked, trying to figure out what happened.

He stopped so abruptly that she plowed right into his back. He spun and caught her before she fell.

"No," he said in that same tone. "You did nothing wrong."

"Then why –" she broke off, more confused than ever.

He kissed her again, on the cheek. "I trust I'll see you tomorrow."

In the few seconds it took for her to clear her head he vanished into the crowd. *Men. Who needs them?* She returned to her table. Emmie was still there, but Cole wasn't. He'd stopped by, because there was a glass of water in front of her seat. She took a sip, letting the tart sparkling water cool her parched throat.

"Cole saw some people he knew," Emmie explained. "He said he'd be back in a bit."

Nisa nodded.

Emmie grinned. "So, how was your hottie?"

Nisa felt the heat rise to her face again, thankful for the cover of darkness. "He can dance," was all she could come up with.

"Yeah, I could tell. I'm actually kind of jealous he went after you." Emmie fanned herself. "Did you at least get his name?"

"Yeah. It's Ty."

"Ty? Hmm. Maybe he could *tie* you up."

Nisa nearly choked as some of the bubbles went up her nose.

Emmie handed her a napkin. "Are you gonna live?" she asked.

Nisa's throat still burned and her eyes watered. Coughing, she shook her head, then cautiously ventured another sip. Some of the burning eased, but she still couldn't speak.

"Dang, I got spew points on that one."

"You're so mean," Nisa wheezed, still coughing.

Emmie thumped her on the back, which helped a little. Finally the ache eased and she was able to breathe normally again. "I can't believe you said that."

"What?" Emmie held up her hands in mock innocence. "I wouldn't say no to him. And I don't think you should, either." She smirked. "Not after the way he kissed you."

Electricity still zinged through her blood from the brief contact of his lips on hers. "He asked me to meet him for lunch tomorrow."

"You have to go," Emmie demanded.

Nisa flashed a teasing smile as she sipped her water, the bubbles tickling her nose. "I don't *have* to do anything."

"But you want to." Emmie bit into her pineapple garnish.

It wasn't a question. Yes, she did. But she wasn't sure she dared.

Chapter 3

Ty paced the Speedway Club lobby, turning toward the door at the slightest sound. *She's gonna stand me up.* Cup practice hadn't gone exactly as he'd hoped, but he trusted his team to get the car right for knock-out qualifying that afternoon.

"Mornin', Tyson."

Ty looked up to see another racing competitor. "Mornin', Mark."

"You waitin' for someone?"

"Yeah." He looked at his watch. She was fifteen minutes late. His heart plummeted. "But it looks like she's gonna no-show."

"Tyson Patterson stood up by a woman." Mark smirked. "What are the odds?"

Ty wanted to knock the smug look off the other man's face, but he remained calm. Someone standing behind them made a noise, and Ty turned. He recognized the restaurant manager immediately.

"Mr. Patterson, the lady says she's with you?" Lawrence stepped aside, and Nisa appeared.

Ty's pulse thundered. Ever the pragmatic optimist, he hadn't actually anticipated seeing her again, though he still held out hope. She took a tentative step toward him, and he discovered she was prettier than he'd remembered. Her coppery hair coiled over her shoulders, and her eyes were a brilliant green. Her figure, while still fashionable, was curvier than most of the women in his acquaintance.

"Did you still want to share lunch?" she asked.

Her voice was soft, and had a smoky quality to it that caressed his senses. Ty was unable to talk for the first time in forever. A hand clapped him on the shoulder. *Damn it!* Mark had noticed her arrival.

"The great Tyson Patterson, speechless," Mark mocked. "I believe that's a first."

"Get lost," Ty growled at the other driver. He couldn't understand why he suddenly felt protective of the woman in front of him. He nodded to Lawrence, who promptly showed him and Nisa to a table overlooking the track. The Xfinity Series drivers were running their final practice session before qualifying that afternoon.

"I'm sorry I'm late," she said. "I had trouble finding this place."

Ty pushed in her chair before sitting opposite her. "You've never been up here before?"

She shook her head, sending the silky rust-colored curls bouncing about her face.

Lawrence informed them of the specials, then handed them each an opened menu. Ty scanned it quickly, already knowing what he wanted. Nisa took a little more time with hers, and he took advantage to study her a little bit more. Her hair was caught halfway between dark blond and brown with a reddish tinge, and her green eyes glowed.

"Can I start you off with something to drink?" the manager asked.

Nisa looked up from her menu. "I'll take a glass of sparkling mineral water with lemon."

"Sweet tea," said Ty.

Lawrence sent his pencil across the pad in a quick flurry. "Are you ready to order?"

Nisa closed the menu and set it at the edge of the table. "I'll take the Cobb salad with the raspberry vinaigrette."

"Are you sure you don't want more time?" Ty asked, mildly surprised by her selection.

Nisa shook her head.

"I'll have the bacon cheeseburger with a side of steamed vegetables," Ty said. "No fries, please."

"Of course, sir." Lawrence jotted their orders, then took the menus and left them alone.

"Is it normal for the restaurant manager to wait tables?" Nisa asked.

"Not usually, but Lawrence and I go back about two years," Ty explained. "He takes great pride in caring for his high-profile clientele."

"Why is that?"

"Because he knows racers, car owners and track officials are on a tight schedule, and he does an amazing job of making sure the kitchen staff stays focused while ensuring the NASCAR members get taken care of quickly." He folded his hands and rested his elbows on the table. "Please, tell me more about you."

The Xfinity Series drivers rocketed past the grandstands, the noise deadened by soundproof glass. Nisa shrugged and looked out over the racetrack. "There isn't much to tell."

"Where did you grow up?" he asked, not giving up easily.

"Darlington. You?"

That surprised him. She had little trace of Southern accent in her beautiful voice. Unlike him. "Kingsport, Tennessee."

A smile flickered across her full, kissable lips. Suddenly he wanted another taste. He thought about it when a waitress stopped by and placed their drinks on the table. The spell dissipated. He mourned the loss of one opportunity, but vowed he wouldn't miss any more. "Where do you live now?" he asked.

"Wisconsin."

"I bet it gets cold during the winter." He rolled his eyes and mentally kicked himself in the ass. *Way to go, moron. She probably thinks you're an idiot.*

That ghost smile flickered again. "We even get snow."

"Where in Wisconsin do you live? What do you do?" He fired the questions at her, his innate curiosity getting the better of him.

"La Crosse. I'm a jewelry designer at a small family-run firm."

"Nice." He took a sip of his drink.

"Yes," she said. "I think it is."

"When you said Darlington, I assumed you meant South Carolina." At her nod, he asked, "What made you decide to move from there to Wisconsin?"

Her eyes grew sad and she faced the glass again. "Personal reasons." Sighing, she turned back to him. "What do you do?"

"I work with cars." He didn't exactly lie, but he didn't tell her the whole truth, either. He suspected she was doing the same.

"You're a mechanic? So was my dad."

He didn't correct her assumption. "Tell me more about him."

She shrugged. "He died when I was ten, and I moved to La Crosse."

She looked out the window one more time. He couldn't say for certain what it was she was looking at, but she seemed to be fixated on the wall in turn three. And unless he was mistaken, her eyes misted. He let the silence stretch between them as he pondered the information she'd given him.

"What about the rest of your family?" She sipped her water. "You said your mother's a professional dancer, and that your brother is following in her footsteps, so to speak. Do you have any other siblings?"

Ty laughed. "No. My parents had a difficult time raisin' two hellion boys as it was."

"Hellions, huh?"

He chuckled. "My mother swears we're the reason her hair turned gray at the young age of thirty-four."

"So while your mom was teaching you and your brother how to dance, what was your father doing?" she asked.

"My father's an HVAC technician." He smiled. "They both still live in Kingsport, and they're just as much in love now as they were when they married thirty-five years ago."

"That's amazing."

"My favorite relative is my grandmother." He grinned. "She's eighty-five years old, and she's still as spunky as ever."

Nisa's eyes glittered. "Tell me about her."

"She lives in a tiny house my parents built for her in their huge backyard, which she turned into an amazing garden." He imagined his blue-and-silver-haired grandmother puttering around amidst a sea of roses in every color available. "She used to love red, but since I've been racin' Cup she switched to wearin' my team colors. She completely updated her wardrobe every time I switched rides. Now she wears mostly blue dresses with her favorite blue-patterned scarf and silver earrings. And on Sundays she carries a silver handbag and wears silver shoes."

"She sounds like a gem." She sipped from her glass again. "Is she where you got your lead foot?"

"Actually yes." He chuckled. "She still has her license, and thinks she's Mario Andretti as she drives her friends to their weekly bridge club meetings. She's the one who gave me driving lessons."

Nisa laughed, the musical sound wafting over him.

"Tiny house, huh?"

"Yeah. It's easy for her to move around in, and she can still be close to her family."

Their food arrived minutes later. She tucked into her salad, which sprawled across the entire plate. He sat back and watched her enjoy the first few bites, realizing how refreshing it was to be with a woman who liked to eat. Her eyes closed and she made appreciative noises in the back of her throat. Lust hit him hard in the gut, and he barely suppressed his moan.

Her eyes flew to his as awareness zinged between them. The pretty blush spread across her cheekbones again, dusting them with a rosy glow. She lowered her eyes to her food, though it didn't break the spell she'd woven around him.

Lawrence chose that moment to stop by their table. "How is everything so far?"

"Excellent," Ty said, though he hadn't even touched his plate.

Lawrence nodded in approval. "Please don't hesitate to ask if you need anything else."

"Thank you." Ty dismissed the manager.

Nisa continued eating, though with less gusto.

Ty cut his burger in half and took a bite. He rarely indulged in red meat anymore, but this was a special occasion. The pretty lady across from him had kept his head spinning since the moment he'd asked her to dance.

Their conversation was stilted and forced but he still liked being with her, so he didn't mind that her answers to his questions were monosyllabic. He couldn't remember when he had enjoyed the company of a beautiful woman more after having done so little with her. He still felt the chemistry sizzling between them, and he could tell she felt it too. He caught her giving him covert glances. Both times she'd blushed and looked away. Once again his curiosity got the better of him. "Tell me, Nisa. What is so fascinating about Turn Three?"

"No – nothing." She turned back to face him, though their eyes didn't connect.

"I think you spent more time starin' across the track than you did talkin' with me." Her whole face turned red, and he regretted embarrassing her. "I'm sorry. I didn't mean to make you uncomfortable."

The waitress came and cleared their plates. Both declined dessert. He had practice again in twenty minutes, and he was sure she had other plans, too, so he requested the check.

"This whole place makes me uncomfortable," Nisa finally confided softly.

"As in…what?" he prompted. "The racetrack?"

"It's my first time back since …" she trailed off. "Since forever."

Ty thought she was going to say something else, but she gave no clues to her thoughts. He didn't say anything more. He figured they'd learned enough about each other for their first date and he didn't want to put any undue pressure on her. After the manager brought the bill, Ty took a quick glance and passed over his credit card. A few minutes later Lawrence returned with a receipt and he signed the slip. "Let me take you back to the infield."

"I – I'd like that." Nisa smiled for the first time since their meeting in the lobby, and once again the urge to kiss her overwhelmed him.

Ty helped her stand and placed his hand on the small of her waist. They descended the elevator to the main lobby, where his car waited to take them back to the infield. The drive was uneventful, both of them sitting in the back seat of the luxury sedan.

He held her hand on the seat between them, his thumb stroking along the soft skin of her wrist. "I'd like to see you again."

"I – I'm not sure how that's possible."

Ty felt her moving away from him, both physically and emotionally. "Am I mistaken? Didn't you have a nice time?"

She nodded emphatically as they emerged from beneath the track's surface. "I did," she insisted. "I'm not sure I'm ready to date again."

"Why not?" he asked, his voice a bit harsh. She flinched again, and he softened his tone. "I really like spendin' time with you, Nisa, and I would love it if you'd give me more of your time." He inhaled, held it, then slowly breathed out. "I haven't been able to stop thinkin' about you," he confided. "Especially the way you felt in my arms while we danced. And I would very much like to see you again."

Nisa gasped sharply and turned to face him across the seat as the driver moved through the infield toward the private motor coach lot. "I – I feel the same about you."

She lowered her gaze. "But I'm leaving Monday. I – spending more time together isn't a good idea."

Ty locked his gaze with hers and brushed his lips over her knuckles once, twice, three times before twining her fingers with his. "At least give me the chance to change your mind."

"Here we are, sir, miss." The driver halted the car in front of Cole Forester's RV.

The reminder of his rival evaporated the undercurrent swirling between them.

Nisa freed her hand from his grasp and unbuckled her seatbelt with clumsy fingers. "That's not a good idea, Ty." She reached for the door handle. Before he could stop her, she was out of the car. "Because I'm afraid you *would* be able to change my mind. Enjoy your weekend."

She closed the door, then disappeared into the motor coach.

Ty sat back in his seat, stunned. First, he couldn't believe that she didn't know who he was. And second, he'd been turned down by a woman for the first time in his adult life. He chuckled mirthlessly.

"Is everything all right, sir?" the driver asked.

Ty shook his head. "Yeah. Fine. Take me back to my hauler."

"Yes, sir." The driver pulled out of the lot and headed for the garage.

Chapter 4

Nisa still felt the tingle of Ty's lips on her hand, though it was barely a caress. Worse, he left her aching for more. She touched her fingertips to her mouth, the warm strength of his fingers still lingered on hers, as she slipped inside the Zephyr and reset the security code.

"How was your date?" Emmie asked from the recliner where she was working on her Celtic blackwork napkins.

Nisa walked up the steps into the living area and flopped onto the sofa. "I think it went well enough." She gave her friend a half-smile. "Though he called me out for being distracted. I couldn't stop staring at turn three where my dad hit."

"Honey, if I had a man that hot, I wouldn't be able to keep my eyes away from him." Emmie sobered, lowering her embroidery hoop to her lap. "But, I guess, if I had to deal with the emotions you're going through right now, I'd probably be distracted too."

Nisa smirked. "I never thought I'd find the courage to come back here again." She sighed, leaning back against the cushions. "Remind me to never date a stock car driver. Having my brother race is bad enough."

Emmie looked up from her needlework. "Not to mention the conflict of interest."

"Huh?" Nisa furrowed her brow.

"Dating your brother's competitor," she clarified. "Not knowing who to cheer for. Divided loyalties."

"Yeah." Nisa sighed again. "Remind me to never date a stock car driver."

"Will do." Emmie sat back again, focusing on the needle in her hand. "But what if Mr. Hotness turns out to be the one?"

"Oh. I hadn't thought of that. He did say he worked with cars, but…" Nisa trailed off.

"Well, there's one way to find out." Emmie slipped the needle through the fine weave of the napkin and set it in her quilted craft bag. "Does Cole have a computer?"

"I don't even know if the Zephyr is hooked up for wireless access."

"This rig's probably equipped with everything, as luxurious as it is." Emmie pointed out. "Wait a sec. We don't need a computer." She dug her phone from her purse on the floor next to her craft bag. "What's his name?"

"Ty."

"Last name?"

"Peterson? Patterson?" Nisa frowned. "Something like that."

Emmie typed furiously on the touch-screen of her smartphone. "Here he is. Tyson Patterson. Thirty-six years old. Driver of the forty-five car on the Monster Energy Cup series."

Nisa let out an unladylike curse, slamming her fist into the cushion. "I knew he was holding out on me!"

Emmie shot her a curious glance. "You know him?"

"I know *of* him. He's Cole's fiercest rival."

Compassion shone from Emmie's eyes. "What are you going to do?"

"Avoid him as much as possible, I guess." Though she wasn't sure she wanted to.

"You wouldn't."

"Em, he's a stock car driver." Nisa threw her hands up in exasperation and hauled herself off the sofa, crossing to the other side of the sitting area. "I can't handle having to deal with what happened to my dad all over again. Cole says he races for Dad's honor and memory. And he can't think about what happened."

"It's all *you* can think about."

"Yes!" Nisa shouted.

"Sheesh. Okay, calm down." Emmie stood up and went over to Nisa, grabbing her upper arms and guiding her back to the sofa. "Sit down before you hurt yourself."

"Shut up." But Nisa couldn't summon any irritation at her friend. She didn't have the emotional energy for it.

"So, what are you gonna do?" Emmie repeated.

"Well, since we're leaving Monday and he'll be doing racing stuff all weekend, it shouldn't be a problem to avoid him. I'll tell Cole that my anxiety is too much and I can't handle going out at night."

"You know he won't buy it, right?"

"He'll have to."

"Nisa, do you want to see Tyson again?" Emmie asked softly.

"Yes. No." Nisa shook her head. "I don't know what to do anymore. I want to get through this weekend without feeling like I'm going to get sick every time I hear a race motor."

"So watching qualifying is out of the question?"

"You can." Nisa shrugged. "I'm going to lie down for a while."

"Okay." Emmie flicked on the television behind the driver's seat and tuned in the racing.

Nisa heard the engine roar as she went through the galley kitchen and into the back bedroom. Flopping onto the bed, she closed her eyes and sighed. "How can I feel so strongly about Ty, Angela?" she said out loud. "He's Cole's fiercest rival. How can we possibly make a relationship work?"

Her heart ached because her sister wasn't there to help her. She was no closer to any answers and as she drifted to sleep, visions of Ty flashed behind her closed eyelids.

****

Ty strode down the center aisle of his hauler and grabbed the blue-and-silver fire suit hanging in his locker. He changed for qualifying and stepped out into the bright North Carolina sunlight, shielding his eyes from the intensity of the rays. He was dismayed to discover that his focus was more on Nisa than his qualifying run.

"How was your date?"

The voice of his crew chief startled Ty out of his thoughts. "It was nice."

"Was she the mystery woman you were dancing with last night?" Pete Haskins asked as they headed for the garage across from the haulers.

Ty nodded. "Her name is Nisa."

"Unusual name."

"Unusual woman. But she kept more of her focus out there." He pointed to turn three. "She seems skittish. Like she's nervous about somethin'."

"What'd she say?"

"Well…" Ty thought back to their lunch conversation. He'd been so busy trying to figure out why she was so selective with her answers that he didn't really pay much attention to her words. "She said this was her first time back to the track in twenty years. Which doesn't make sense, because she can't be older than twenty-seven."

"Hmm. Can't be who I thought she was then." Pete appeared lost in thought.

Ty punched him lightly in the arm. "I think you're losin' your touch, old man."

"Me?" Pete returned the punch. "You're the one who couldn't follow through with a pretty woman. Maybe we oughtta knock you off that pedestal."

"Cut me some slack. I just met her last night."

"Yeah. And the Tyson Patterson I knew would've had her bagged and tagged in thirty seconds flat."

"That's crude," he scolded Pete.

"Yeah, well, so were you." Pete's expression softened. "So what changed?"

Ty leaned against the car as the crew swarmed, getting it ready for qualifying. He breathed in deep, enjoying the smells of grease, oil, and rubber permeating the air. He exhaled slowly, letting the tension in his body go as he released his breath. "I wish I knew."

The air guns whirred as the crew put the tires back on the car, then removed the jack stands and lowered it to the concrete slab. Ty followed as the crew pushed the car onto pit road.

As Ty's crew got the car into qualifying position other crews pushed cars to the line-up, and others were already there making as many last-second adjustments as they could. A few die-hard fans speckled the stands, but it wasn't unusual for qualifying. Sunday's race was a sell-out, which was all that mattered.

Ty climbed in through the window and hooked all the safety equipment into place, before pulling on his helmet. Pete hooked it to the neck restraint device, then secured the whole assembly to the tether attached to the headrest and connected the air hose.

"Thanks, Pete."

Pete grunted as Ty secured the wheel to the central hub and gave it a good yank before pulling on his driving gloves. Pete secured the window net and stepped behind the wall.

"How's the radio?" Pete's voice crackled in his ear.

Ty reached for the button on the wheel next to his right thumb. "Loud and clear."

"Copy that. Roll-off's in one minute."

"Ten-four." Ty released the button and leaned back in his custom-molded carbon-fiber seat, enjoying the last few seconds of silence. He closed his eyes and held his breath. Focused his energy. He exhaled, releasing the rest of his pent-up tension as he opened his eyes.

"Fire 'em up." Pete's instruction came across the radio.

Ty reached to his left and flipped the toggle switches. Seven-hundred and fifty horses roared to life beneath him. The vibrations quaked the chassis, and the shifting lever almost shook out of his hand as he reached for it. His grip was firm as he shoved the shifter into first gear and popped the clutch, letting the car roll. The first round was fifteen minutes, and Ty wasted no time in getting up to full race speed heading down the front stretch and taking the green flag. He drafted with his teammate Dominick Sands into turns one and two and stayed on his bumper down the backstretch.

Ty and Dom pulled up fast on the inside of Cole Forester. Ty glanced quickly, seeing Cole running by himself with a long train of cars coming up behind them.

"You're fifth, twenty-eight-point-four-two seconds," Pete relayed.

"Ten-four." Ty released the button as he raced to the bumper of his teammate. Ty pulled to the left, ducking beneath the black-and-silver car on the low side of the track. He cleanly sailed by Dom, then pulled up in front of him heading down the front-stretch. He saw the black and red flags flying high above the track.

"You're up to second, behind the sixty-three car. Twenty-seven-point-eight-one," Pete relayed.

"How did Cole get faster than me?" Ty asked, confused.

"He's in a cluster. We're in the next round. Bring it in."

"Ten-four." Ty slowed on the backstretch and pulled onto pit lane before making the hard left turn into the garage, letting his crew take care of the car. He unhooked the safety gear and climbed out, discussing with his crew how the car handled and what improvements needed to be made for the second run.

Seven minutes later, the adjustments made, Ty climbed back into his car with the other top twenty-three competitors vying for the pole. "I hate this qualifying format," he muttered as he flipped the switches again. He pulled into his starting position before shutting the motor down again.

"Sit tight. Be ready to go with one minute and twenty seconds left."

"Ten-four." Adrenaline coursed through him, making his hands tremble.

"Thirty seconds," Pete counted down.

Ty began the countdown in his head.

"Ten seconds."

Ty reached over and fired the motor in anticipation of rolling off for the first of two qualifying laps.

"Go, go, go!"

Ty popped the clutch and drove off pit road onto the track for a warmup lap. He came up to speed and had a good head of steam coming off turn four onto the front stretch. The official waved the green flag and Ty sailed into turn one for the first of two laps he planned to run. He got out front early and pulled away from the rest of the pack.

"Twenty-seven-point-four-nine." Pete relayed the first lap time.

"Ten-four." Ty concentrated on hitting the same marks on the second lap as he did the first and crossed the start/finish line.

"One more lap. You crossed the line before the time ran out. Stay strong. Twenty-seven-point-two-six."

Ty kept the throttle mashed to the floor as he headed down the backstretch into turn three. The rear end fishtailed and the car almost jumped from beneath him.

"Whoa, girl!" He sawed the wheel back and forth, trying to keep the car off the wall, but he lost too much time and the last lap ended up as a wash. He finished the lap and tapped the brake, slowing down to enter the pits off turn four.

"You're still good enough to go for the pole. What happened?" Pete asked.

"She almost went around on me heading into three," Ty explained. "Tighten me up just a tick for the last run."

"Copy that. Seven minutes to pole run."

"Ten-four." Ty braked in his garage bay and let his crew go to work on the car as he removed his helmet.

"Careful in turn three." Pete stuck his head into the driver's window.

"Ya think?" Ty muttered beneath his breath.

"Same as before. Wait until my cue to go. You can get two laps run with one-twenty left on the clock."

Ty nodded. With two minutes left on the clock, he put his helmet on one more time and drove up to the starting line at the exit of pit road, then killed the motor.

"Timin' clock startin' now. Wait for my cue," his crew chief instructed again.

Ty fired the motor. To his chagrin, the sixty-three car was in his mirror. Cole had made it to the final round, too.

"Thirty seconds," Pete said.

Same as before, Ty counted down in his head while the car idled around him. He shoved the shifter into first, keeping both the brake and clutch squashed to the floorboards.

"Three … two … go, go, go!" Pete commanded.

Ty shifted his foot from the brake to the gas and quickly and rolled off pit lane one last time. The adjustments were perfect and his car was on rails. He hit his marks. Unfortunately, so did Cole. They were side-by-side coming back around to complete their second lap as the black and red flags waved above the track.

"Twenty-seven-point-one-eight," Pete said in his ear. "Good enough for second."

"Who got first?" Ty asked.

"Cole nicked you by three one-hundredths."

Damn! Ty was hoping they'd finish the other way around. *As long as I finish ahead of him on Sunday.*

He steered onto pit lane and drove straight to the garage, pulling into his stall before cutting the engine. Disengaging the safety equipment, he climbed from the car.

"Everyone's makin' such a big deal of turn three," Ty mumbled as they walked back to his hauler for post-qualifying debriefing.

"Well, considerin' what happened twenty years ago, and what NASCAR's doin' this weekend, it's not surprisin'," Pete commented.

Ty's curiosity got the better of him. "What happened?"

"You can't tell me you ain't never heard the story of Gary Forester," Pete derided.

That caught Ty off-guard. "Cole's old man?"

"Yeah. He was headin' into turn three two-thirds of the way through the Memorial Day Classic when his car broke loose and slammed nose-first into the wall. Somethin' failed, and he died on impact." Pete shuddered as they entered the hauler.

"Just like Dale Earnhardt at Daytona," Ty said.

"Exactly. Except it happened right here, in our own backyard."

"And NASCAR has the brilliant idea to do a tribute to him before the race on Sunday," Ty guessed, following his crew chief's direction of thought.

"Rumor has it they flew his daughter in for the event, too. It'll be the first time she'll step foot at this place since it happened. She wasn't here when Gary wrecked, but Cole was."

A pang of sympathy shot through Ty. He couldn't imagine watching his dad get killed like that. Granted it was a freak accident, but it still must've been hard on Cole and his sister. A shiver of foreboding snaked its way down his spine as they entered the conference room at the front of the hauler for the meeting.

Chapter 5

Fingers of crimson and gold crept across the inky sky, the stars winking off like street lamps as dawn slowly pushed away the night. Nisa groaned, and snuggled deeper into the blankets, wishing she could just go back to sleep.

Despite the king-sized bed and satin sheets, her racing thoughts prevented her from getting more than a couple hours' sleep at a time. Groaning, she shoved the blankets aside and padded to the window, pulling back the drapes. She was no closer to figuring out her tumultuous emotions than she'd been after her brief conversation with Emmie after her date with Ty.

"I could use your help, Angela," she whispered to the rising sun. "I can easily see myself falling for him." She didn't want to, but feared her heart had control over her head.

Though the sun cleared the horizon, it had yet to breach the grandstands when Nisa dropped the curtain and headed for the bathroom. After brushing her teeth she opened the door and turned toward the bedroom.

"Morning," Emmie said from the kitchen booth.

Nisa jumped. "I didn't expect you to be up so early."

"You, either." Emmie raised her coffee mug in salute. "I heard you moving around last night. Couldn't sleep?"

"Not really." Nisa popped a pod into the single-serve coffee maker Cole never left home without and poured water into the back of the machine.

"What was it?" Emmie sipped her coffee. "Your dad? Or Ty?"

"Probably both." Nisa shrugged as she waited for the coffee to brew. Talking to her sister had been of no help.

Emmie shrugged. "I'm going to miss this when I go back home."

"What?" Nisa gave her friend a curious look from the topic change.

"The gourmet coffee maker. The Idiot Twins will never let me have one."

Nisa knew her friend was having problems with her family, but she hadn't realized things had deteriorated so badly. The machine turned off and she carried her mug to the booth, sliding onto the bench across from Emmie and laid a hand across hers. "Well, since you're the only one working, I don't see how it's any of their business."

Emmie withdrew her hand.

Nisa sensed the older woman shutting down emotionally at the same time and silence stretched between them as they sipped their coffee. There may be fifteen years between them, but they didn't let the age difference stop them from becoming the best of friends. "I know you don't like talking about them, but if you ever need a break, my door is always open." Glancing at the clock, she slid from the booth and emptied her mug. "I'm going for a walk. Would you like to come with me?"

Emmie's repudiating grimace was partially hidden behind her mug. "Maybe next time."

Tamping down her frustration, Nisa returned to Cole's room and threw some clothes on the bed. She was in the process of braiding her hair into a single plait down her back when a pounding sound caught her attention.

"Nisa?" Emmie called behind the closed door moments later. "Someone's here to see you."

Nisa groaned, wishing she could go back to bed.

"Nisa?" Emmie called again.

"Tell them I'll be out in a few," she mumbled.

"Okay."

Nisa didn't care who was waiting out there for her. She changed from her pajamas covered in Cole's sponsor logos to a pair of black sweatpants emblazoned with the La

Crosse baseball team's logo on the side, a black tank top, and a purple velour running jacket. She then shoved her feet into a pair of purple and white Asics. Once her visitor left she planned to take a jog around the infield. After a quick glance in the mirror she strode to the sitting area.

And stopped dead.

The subject of her dreams was sitting on her brother's sofa chatting with her best friend.

"Hello, Nisa," said Ty, rising from the emerald-green cushion when he saw her.

"Ty," she returned. "What are you doing here?"

"I've come to ask you to be my date for the Gary Forester Memorial brunch," he said.

Spots danced in Nisa's vision and she felt light-headed.

"Nisa?" Concern clouded his eyes. "Are you all right?"

"N – no. I mean yes, I'm fine." She took a deep breath. Up to now she'd managed to keep things light and uncomplicated with Ty. Somehow she *knew* that having him escort her to the brunch was going to shove things into the 'way beyond complicated' zone. Especially since he was Cole's biggest rival.

"Nisa, didn't Cole say something yesterday about wanting you to go with him?" Emmie asked.

Nisa thanked her lucky stars for Emmie's presence. She couldn't have asked for a better person or a more loyal friend. "I think you're right," she said to her friend and turned back to Ty. "I – I'm sorry, Ty, but I better honor my commitment to Cole. I'll see you there, though?"

"Count on it." His voice was flat, his face expressionless. He turned to leave, but then did something Nisa didn't expect. He stormed over to her and, cupping her face in his strong calloused hands, gave her the most passionate kiss she'd ever had in her life. "He can't give you what I can, darlin'."

Nisa stood completely dazed as Ty left the Zephyr under a cloud of anger and unfinished business. Emmie finally jolted her out of her stupor a minute later.

"Oh my," Emmie said, fanning herself with her hand. "You lucky bitch. He's *HOT!*"

Nisa's knees threatened to buckle, and she collapsed onto the sofa. "I don't know what to do," she wailed. "He's a racecar driver, and Cole's toughest competitor. I don't want to want him like I do!"

All amusement fled from Emmie's pretty features. "Nisa, are you falling for Ty?"

Nisa closed her eyes and flopped her head against the back of the couch, accidentally bonking it against the window ledge. "Ow!" She rubbed the sore spot as Emmie snickered. "Honestly, I don't know at this point. We've had time to get to know each other. But I still haven't told him my last name, and he doesn't know I'm Cole's sister."

"Yeah, that does complicate things," Emmie agreed.

"I wish Shayna was here. She'd be able to give me some ideas on what to do."

"That she could." Emmie yawned and stretched. "Why don't we go for a walk to clear our heads?"

Nisa looked at her friend like she'd grown a second head. As far as she knew, Emmie had never been interested in going on walks with her, even though she'd prodded a few times. "I'd like that. Thank you."

They left the Zephyr a few minutes later, water bottles in hand, as they took a path around that wove through the half-full private motor coach lot. Because most of the teams were headquartered not far from the speedway, she knew most of the drivers had probably slept in their own beds last night.

There were scores of gated communities along the shores of Lake Norman north of Downtown Charlotte, and Nisa knew that most of the drivers had homes in those communities. Cole included. Multi-million-dollar sprawling estates with private docks and beaches. Nisa had chosen to stay at the track because she feared chickening out if she commuted from Cole's place.

They returned to Cole's RV and Nisa punched the security code into the keypad, unlocking the door. "Go ahead and shower first. I'll make something to eat."

"Thanks." Emmie grabbed a sheet of paper towel from the roll next to the sink and mopped the sweat from her face, then headed for the bathroom.

After she heard the water running, Nisa took some eggs, ham and shredded cheese from the refrigerator and set them on the counter next to the stove. Grabbing a frying pan and the butter next, she heated up the pan for an omelet. She rummaged through the fridge again and found some fresh spinach. She added it to the pile and fixed the omelet.

When she dumped it on the plate the cheese oozed out the sides and the bottom was golden brown. The water stopped running the moment she brought the first bite to her lips. Sliding from the booth, she crossed the small kitchen and snagged another plate from the cabinet over the counter. She cut the omelet in half and dumped a portion onto the clean plate for Emmie. Then she savored the first bite.

"That smells amazing," Emmie said as she joined Nisa in the kitchenette.

Nisa handed her the plate and a fork. "Dig in."

"Thanks."

Nisa was famished, and took no time at all to finish off her portion. "I'm gonna shower. Leave the dishes in the sink. We'll get them later."

Emmie nodded and Nisa disappeared in the back.

****

Shortly before ten, Nisa and Emmie entered the white tent located right outside the track in the hospitality village where the memorial brunch was scheduled. Only select media were invited inside, and no one from the general public was allowed. The event was way more than her father would've wanted.

She knew it was an honor that the general manager wanted to pay tribute to her father's legacy with such grandeur, but she could hear her father's voice in her ear stating that it was way too flashy for him. A tear trickled down her cheek, and she flicked it away with her fingertip.

"Are you okay?" Cole asked from by her side.

Nisa nodded. "I miss him."

"I do, too." He squeezed her hand. "He would've loved this."

"Oh, please." Nisa rolled her eyes. "He would've said it was too fancy, that he didn't deserve this."

Cole laughed. "I think you may be right." He squeezed her hand again, and she felt the reassurance in his grip. "They put us up front."

She grimaced. "Of course they did."

Nisa let Cole guide her through the sea of people toward the raised dais at the front of the white tent, thanking this person and that person for being there to honor her father. As she reached the front, she felt the magnetic pull that she only felt when Ty was around. Her head inexorably turned in his direction. Their gazes locked across the crowded space. She gasped and turned away, horrified by the anger blazing in his eyes.

Cole grabbed two flutes from a passing waiter and pressed one into her hand. Nisa looked at him, puzzled. He chuckled. "It's orange juice."

Nisa relaxed a bit and took a sip of the tart liquid. Yep, straight-up OJ. She smiled at her brother, taking her cue from him as they mingled with the attendees, thanking them for coming to the event.

"Your father was one of the greats," the man next to Nisa said. "I consider it a privileged to have raced against him."

"Thank you, Richard," she responded. "I'm sure he felt the same about you."

Stories were swapped over the next half-hour about how Gary Forester was such a wonderful man, and how he raced hard but clean. A gentleman to the end. The sound of someone tapping a microphone through loudspeakers caught her attention, and she turned toward the podium.

"Good morning," said Vincent Kincade from behind the mic. "And thank you all for coming to this memorable occasion. There are a couple people we need to give a special thanks to. Cole, if you'll join me up here, please."

Nisa watched as her brother made his way to the dais.

"Cole, it's my honor, and privilege, to say thank you for everything you've done for the sport of NASCAR. Your father would be proud of all your accomplishments."

"Thank you, Mr. Kincade," Cole said into the microphone, then stepped back. Applause rippled through the crowd.

"Let's get your sister up here," Vincent said. "This is as much for her as it is for you."

Nisa gasped, her eyes snapping first to Cole's, then to Ty's. Blood drained from his face. *Oh god.* She made her way up to the front of the room and joined Cole at the table, nodding to Vincent at the podium. Sitting in the chair to Cole's right, she pasted a smile onto her lips that felt as fake as she did. Looking around the space, she recognized some of the guys her father had raced against twenty years earlier.

Guys who raced for many years before turning to television or radio broadcasting analysts. Racers who'd gotten into horrific wrecks on the track and lived to tell the tales. She only wished her father could be among them.

A projection screen had been propped up in the opposite corner across from where Nisa sat. She turned her chair to face it. Suddenly images of her father filled the screen, and a well-known retired racer's voice poured from the speakers, the narrative both humorous and moving.

Gary Forester's life was chronicled in the video, and Nisa found herself reaching for the napkin next to her plate. She dabbed her eyes, wiping away tears of sadness in one moment, then tears of laughter in the next. There were so many people who loved her father, and it warmed her heart that his legacy would live on in this amazing sport.

When the video ended, Nisa's throat closed up with emotion, and waved for Emmie to come up to the table as the rest of the audience applauded.

"What's wrong?" Emmie asked, concerned.

"Will you sit up here with us?" she asked brokenly. "Please."

Emmie sat in the chair next to Nisa.

"Thank you," she whispered.

Emmie hugged her. "You're welcome."

"And now, ladies and gentlemen, to say a few words, here's Gary's son, Cole." Vincent's voice boomed from the loudspeakers, and the applause picked up again as Cole stepped up to the mic.

"Thank you, everyone," Cole welcomed the crowd. "My father would have been honored and humbled if he were here with us today. Gary Forester had been a simple man, living by a set of simple rules. He never took favors, and never asked for any. He didn't want to owe anybody anything. Except when it came to his racecars. He had no problem persuading wealthy business owners to invest in his stock car, and his racing career. There were a few DNF's along the way, but for the most part Gary was a closer." He scanned the interior, his speech slow and controlled. "I knew him as Dad. The man I wanted to beat on and off the track. The competitor who pointed out my mistakes with lightning-quick efficiency, but the father who was equally quick to give a pat on the back for a job well-done."

Nisa dabbed her eyes with the napkin as Cole continued.

"Losing him was one of the hardest things I've ever had to face in my life," he said, "both personally and professionally. My father, my mentor. My inspiration. I know he would be proud of both my sister and me today, in how far we've both come in our lives, and I know he's smiling down on us from Heaven."

Nisa sniffed, dabbing her eyes again. She had a speech prepared, but she wasn't sure if she'd make it through without bawling. Emmie rubbed her back. Nisa took comfort in the contact.

"I remember when, as a kid, I told Dad I wanted to race," Cole continued with his speech. "He said, 'Son, you can race as long as you earn it.' I'll never forget those words. Hell, I think I'm *still* trying to earn it!" Subdued chuckles rippled through the audience. He let it die down before he continued. "But I'll never forget the day he died,

crashing head-on into the turn three wall right here at the
Charlotte Motor Speedway. I still get chills every time I
slip into my car at this track, because I know he's here.
Somewhere. Watching. Guiding. Like he has my entire
life." He paused, and Nisa watched him scan the sea of
people.

She did the same moments later, looking
everywhere except at Ty. Though she could feel his gaze
burning a hole into her flesh. Cole continued his speech,
and she watched him again.

"I miss my dad, mostly because he was my dad, but
I know his death wasn't in vain. We now have softer walls
around all the tracks, and the cars are designed to better
absorb the impact of the crashes. The safety innovations
that have transpired in the last quarter-century have come
about because of him. Those same innovations have saved
my hide a number of times, and I'm sure my fellow
competitors can attest the same." Cole cleared his throat.

"But, as I said, my father was a simple man who
lived by a simple code of honesty, integrity and honor. If he
were here today … let's face it. If he were here today, we
wouldn't be here. But if he were here, he'd humbly say
'thank you,' then blend into the crowd and do his best to
whoop us all on the track during the race."

Cole smiled wryly, once again letting the ripples of laughter dissipate. "However, because he isn't here to say it himself, please allow me to do it for him. NASCAR meant a lot to him. It was his life, his work. His family. He had nothing but the utmost respect for every competitor on the track, even as he tried beating them at the same time. I know that everyone in this room misses him as much as I do. Thank you."

The audience shot to their feet and a thunderous applause roared through the tent.

Nisa gave up on the napkin and let the tears flow freely down her face.

Chapter 6

Ty was furious. Still reeling at the identity of his brunette goddess, he wasn't sure if he was madder at her for not telling him or at himself for not figuring her out.

"Helluva surprise, eh?" Pete clapped a beefy hand on Ty's shoulder. "Who'd've thought you'd fall for your rival's sister?"

Ty grunted, desperately needing something stronger than the orange juice in his hand. But NASCAR would probably park him if he had alcohol before a race. He didn't have a win yet this season, and was still trying to get himself into the Playoffs. His car was dialed in, and his hopes for tonight's event were high.

Ty finally got up and made his way around the room to where Cole and Nisa stood near the entrance to the tent and shook his competitor's hand. "Great speech."

"Thanks."

Ty nodded, then turned to the woman by Cole's side. "Pleasure to see you again, Nisa."

"Ty." Her voice was cool, composed. Like she was pretending he hadn't kissed her senseless a few hours earlier.

That pissed him off more. He wanted to muss her hair and smear her lipstick, but he forced himself to remain calm. However, he did catch the look of surprise that flickered briefly through Cole's eyes. Ty had a feeling Little Sister had some explaining to do. He wasn't sure if he wanted to be there for it or if he was better off leaving well enough alone. Too bad his head and other parts of his anatomy couldn't agree on the best decision at the moment.

Ty could tell that Cole and Nisa were close by the protectiveness he displayed for his sister. For the first time since he'd climbed into a Cup car, he saw his rival as more than just another competitor. Nisa made him more human. His respect for Cole increased a few notches.

He couldn't imagine what was going through Cole's mind, but he had a feeling it wasn't pleasant. Ty couldn't blame him. If he'd had a sister like Nisa, he'd be as protective of her. And he sure as hell wouldn't want his archenemy sniffing around her. He had a sneaking suspicion that Cole would probably try taking a shot at him. He'd have to wait and see if it would happen mid-race or off-track. He exchanged a few more awkward pleasantries, though if anyone asked he wouldn't be able to recall any of it. He shook Cole's hand one more time, then returned to where his crew chief was talking to his car owner.

A wry smile twisted his lips. He must be one sick bastard, because his feelings for Nisa refused to let him stay away from her. He left the tent and headed for his hauler. It was too early to change for the race, but he couldn't stay a moment longer.

****

Nisa watched Ty leave, her heart sinking to her toes. She'd caught Cole's questioning glance, and she wasn't sure how she was going to get around appeasing his curiosity without incurring his ire.

"Don't worry about it." Emmie sipped her orange juice from a champagne flute. "You're both consenting adults, and neither of you did anything wrong."

Emmie was right. Nisa sipped from her own gold-rimmed crystal flute.

"Don't they have champagne to mix with the juice?" Emmie asked.

Nisa grinned at the irony. "I thought the same thing. But since most of the guys are in tonight's race, it's probably best they don't."

"Hmm, you're probably right," Emmie conceded, sipping from her glass. "Wouldn't want a bunch of drunk drivers taking the track later."

Nisa sobered. "No, sure wouldn't." Her thoughts returned to her father, as they had many times over the weekend. Ty's angry features filled her vision, and her eyes blurred.

"Are you all right?" Emmie asked.

Nisa shook her head. "I can't help thinking about Ty."

"Ty's such an appropriate name for him. I wouldn't mind *tying* him up."

Nisa smiled, even as heat infused her face. "You're one sick puppy," she accused her friend.

"Thank you." Emmie laughed. "It's nice to be appreciated for one of my finer qualities."

"That's something Shayna would say."

"Who do you think I stole it from?"

They giggled, despite the somber, almost reverent atmosphere that had settled among the remaining crowd.

Cole came over and settled his arm around Nisa's shoulder, cocking a brow at her. "What's so funny?"

"Nothing," Emmie said too quickly.

"We were talking about Shayna," Nisa said to keep Cole from getting suspicious.

Cole nodded, and Nisa hoped he accepted the pseudo-explanation for what it was.

When she followed Cole into his hauler later that morning, she knew her luck had run out as he guided her to the front room and closed the door.

"When were you going to tell me about you and Tyson?" he asked in a light tone.

"There's nothing to tell, Cole," she replied. "He asked me to dance Thursday night, then to lunch on Friday at the Speedway Club. I didn't even know who he was until Friday evening."

"And yesterday?" he prompted, a little more firmly.

"He asked me to meet him after practice." She shrugged. "I don't think he knew who *I* was until this morning."

"You didn't tell him?" His eyebrows shot up in disbelief.

"I told him my name," she said softly. "But I don't think he connected me to you until now." Anxiety shot through her when Cole didn't say anything. "I know how you feel about him, and I don't want to cause any more trouble between you." Nisa broke the lengthening silence.

"I can't decide if I should warn you off of him, or if I should tell you to live your own life," he said at last. "I know you're an adult, capable of making your own decisions."

"But you raised me," she said, understanding. "Old habits die hard."

"Yes, they do." He sighed. "Be careful, okay? I don't want you to get hurt."

"I know, Cole," Nisa hugged him, relief easing her tense posture. "I don't want to get hurt, either."

A knock sounded on the door of the conference room. Cole pulled away from her to answer it.

Zeke, peered from the doorway. "Driver's meeting in fifteen minutes."

"Thanks, man," Cole told his crew chief.

"Will I see you back at the motor coach?" Nisa asked.

Cole shook his head. "I'll probably hang out here until race time, strategizing with Zeke. Will you come with me to the meeting?"

Nisa smiled, putting her hand on Cole's arm. "Of course."

****

Nisa and Emmie were halfway through watching a mildly amusing rom-com two hours later when someone pounded on the door. Nisa checked the security screen – and gasped. Ty – *Tyson Patterson* – was waiting for her to answer, tapping his foot impatiently.

"It's Ty," she whispered to her friend.

Emmie paused the movie. "Let him in. I'll go to the kitchen."

Nisa watched until Emmie was out of sight before opening the door. "Ty. This is –"

His mouth crashed onto hers in a kiss that was as explosive as it was angry. Her lips smashed against her teeth. His fingers anchored hard in her hair. She clutched at his solid biceps as she kissed him back with equal fervor. When she thought she would pass out from lack of oxygen, he pulled back. His fingers stayed twined in her hair. Her lungs burned as she gulped in deep breaths. His breathing was just as rough.

"Tell me that wasn't a farce," he demanded, his voice harsh. "That you didn't play me."

Nisa was still trying to recover from his brutal kiss, but her head popped up. "No!" she denied vehemently. "I would never do that to anyone!"

"Why didn't you tell me?" he bit out, his hands dropping from her hair.

"Tell you what?" Nisa demanded, crossing her arms over her chest and stepping back.

"That you were his sister." Ty glowered at her. "You made me look like a fool."

"No, Ty." She stood her ground this time. "You did that all on your own."

The tension left his body as his shoulders slumped forward and he guided her into the living room where he sat on the sofa opposite her.

"Ty, I want you to leave."

His gaze pleaded with hers. "Not until we clear this up."

"There's nothing to clear up," she countered. "I'm Cole's sister." She bit out a humorless laugh. "It's ironic, really. I didn't know who you were when you asked me to dance."

His head lifted and his brow furrowed. "But Cole –"

"I don't follow NASCAR." She shrugged. "I haven't in a long time."

"Then why did you dance with me?"

Heat flooded her face and she turned away. "Because I thought you were gorgeous." She sighed, deciding to be as brutally honest with him as he'd been with her. "And because you were a welcome distraction in an already stressful weekend."

His hands curled around her arms. "How was I a distraction?"

Nisa jumped. She hadn't heard him move. Her heart raced. "This is my first time back since Dad –" She broke off, fighting tears.

"That explains why you don't follow NASCAR." Ty rubbed his hands gently on her arms, his warm lips caressing her neck.

A shiver snaked through her.

"I'm so sorry, Nisa." He wrapped his arms around her waist and pulled her flush against him, her back to his front. "I didn't realize how difficult coming back would be for you."

Nisa turned in the circle of his arms and threaded her fingers into his silky hair as he drew her lips to his. Instead of demanding a response, he coaxed and seduced. His tongue ran along the seam of her lips. She gasped, and he slipped inside. His tongue glided against hers, sending another shockwave across her nerves.

All she wanted was to immerse herself in the storm that was Tyson Patterson. To forget she was at the track where her father died, and that Ty had been Cole's fiercest rival since their altercation at Bristol three years ago.

The moment she thought she'd cave and respond, he broke off. Her eyelids fluttered open. Regret had replaced the anger in his gaze, and Nisa couldn't decide which was worse.

"Nisa." His voice was raspy with unspent passion. "I want to see you after this weekend."

Her head swam and her eyes burned with unshed tears. Her throat clogged and she couldn't speak. All she could do was shake her head. Ty kissed her again, desire mixed with infinite patience, before he finally released her.

"I'm not goin' away." His voice was weary. He dug his phone from his back pocket, looked at it, then back to her. "I have to leave now, but I'll find you after the race."

Ty gave her another quick, hard kiss before exiting the motor coach.

Stunned, Nisa stood frozen to her spot as she watched him leave. She'd sensed a leashed power beneath the veneer of patience. She shivered again, filled with longing, uncertainty, and a heavy dose of desire.

"That went well, I think." Emmie emerged from her hiding spot in the kitchen. "He really likes you."

Turning to her friend, Nisa frowned. "Do you think so?"

"I do." Emmie grinned. "And judging from that exchange, you really like him too."

Nisa flopped onto the sofa. "There's no point in denying it. Funny thing is, I started falling for him on Friday."

"Before you knew what he did." Emmie sat next to her and rubbed her back in comfort.

"What am I going to do?" Nisa wailed, more to herself than her friend.

"Only you can answer that, hon." Emmie stated the obvious. "Whatever decision you make, follow your heart." She grinned. "If nothing else, enjoy him for the weekend, then walk away tomorrow when we leave."

Nisa stared off into space, mulling over her friend's words. The thought of never seeing Ty again made her heart clench with sadness, but she wasn't sure she could enter the racing world again without fear of history repeating itself.

Chapter 7

Ty stormed into his hauler, fury still raging through him. The rest of his team saw his fierce scowl and scurried as he made his way to the conference room.

"Women troubles?" Pete snickered.

Ty plopped on the sofa and glared at his crew chief, eliciting another amused chuckle from the older man.

Pete sat on the sofa next to him. "Okay. One woman." He sobered. "Does Forester know you're sweet on his sister?"

Ty's chest constricted. Instead of answering his most trusted colleague's question, he countered with one of his own. "When did you know you were in love with Isobel?"

His crew chief didn't hesitate. "Within two minutes of meetin' her."

"So love at first sight exists?"

Pete's weather-beaten face split into a rare grin, his teeth glistening white against his tan skin. "Yeah, it exists. For those who believe, it does."

Ty sighed, some of the tightness in his chest easing. He wanted to know more about Nisa, but he didn't want Pete to think he was pumping for information. "Did you know Cole's dad?"

"I met him a few times." Pete sat forward, resting his elbows on his knees. "But I never really knew him. He was a good man. So's Cole."

"What happened to his daughters?" Ty couldn't contain his curiosity.

"Angela died the year before. AIDS was the rumor, though it was never confirmed. Sweet gal. Liked to party hard, though." Pete leaned back against the sofa. "No one knew what happened to Nisa." He grinned wryly. "Until now."

"She went into hidin'? At ten?" Ty had difficulty believing that.

Pete looked lost in thought for a moment. "I'm not sure if it was hidin' or gettin' away from the circus. Cole drew all the attention onto himself, maybe to keep her safe." Pete sighed. "No one said anythin' 'bout the little girl who'd lost her father. Eventually questions about her stopped. But those of us who were there never forgot about her." He paused again. "He never had a memorial for her or anythin', so I figured she was still alive."

And she hadn't followed racing since. Ty grimaced.

"What is it?" Pete asked softly.

As long as Ty had known him, Pete always had the uncanny ability to pick up on his emotions. "I don't know," Ty replied. "Somethin' she said keeps comin' back to me."

"What was it?"

"That I was a 'distraction in a stressful weekend'." He air-quoted the words that had hurt the most.

Pete chuckled. "Hurt your feelin's, did she?"

Ty shrugged, grimacing. "Yeah. And because of the rivalry with me and Cole, she won't even give us a chance."

"What'd ya expect? Open arms?"

Ty shoved off the sofa, frustrated. "She did at first, so, I guess, yeah. Maybe I did."

"What'd ya mean, she did at first?"

Ty chuckled mirthlessly. "I know why she did."

He paced the floor a couple times, suddenly feeling like a caged tiger. He shoved his hands through his hair. "Damn it!" Nisa had tied him in knots.

"Well?"

Pete's soft word broke into Ty's thoughts, and he paused midstride. A puzzled frown creased his brow. "Well, what?"

"Aren't ya gonna say why?"

"Why what?"

Pete laughed with genuine amusement. "You ain't that old, boy. Ya can't be losin' your memory yet."

Ty could see his crew chief watching him from the corner of his eye.

The old man grinned like a fool. "You must be real hung up on her if'n she got ya goin' in circles."

Smug bastard. Ty had the overwhelming urge to slam his fist through the wall.

"Why's she got ya tied up?"

"She said she didn't know who I was when I asked her to dance Thursday night." Had it only been three days?

"Possible. If'n she don't follow NASCAR." Pete's voice was infuriatingly soft.

Ty was too keyed up to consider it.

Pete rose and strode to the door. "Ty, ya got twenty minutes till driver intros. Cool down, then suit up. See ya on the grid."

Ty looked at the clock and cursed, ramming his fist into the couch cushion. Some of the frustration eased, but a huge weight still pressed against his chest. He changed into his blue-and-silver fire suit, then stepped into the sultry Carolina sunshine.

****

Nisa had fought to keep the tears at bay in front of Ty, but as soon as he left, they slid unheeded down her cheeks.

"Oh, hon." Emmie rubbed her hand over Nisa's shoulders. "Are you okay?"

Nisa sniffled. "Not really." She gave her friend a watery smile. "Didn't I tell you to not let me fall for a NASCAR driver?"

"What does Cole think?"

Emmie's question tore at Nisa's heart. "He has his reservations," she admitted. "But if it's what I want, he won't say no. He wants me to be happy."

"And what do you want?" Emmie asked softly.

"I want Ty," Nisa confessed.

"You love him?"

Nisa felt punched in the gut. She didn't know if what she felt for Ty was love, as she'd never experienced the emotion before, and she wasn't sure if it wasn't the excitement of the forbidden. She only knew she had some heavy thinking to do. She looked at the clock. "We better get ready for the race."

Emmie nodded, and Nisa went back to her borrowed bedroom.

Ten minutes later, their hot passes around their necks, Nisa and Emmie walked to Cole's hauler. Bittersweet emotions bombarded Nisa as she remembered the last time she'd traipsed through Hauler Row. Suddenly the hairs on the back of her neck stood up as a heavy weight rested on her shoulder. Thinking it was Emmie she turned and looked for her friend, who'd stopped at one of the haulers behind her.

"Daddy?" Nisa whispered, a tear trickling down her cheek.

The pressure lifted, and an immense peace flooded her.

"Are you all right?" Emmie caught back up to her and gave her a questioning glance.

Nisa wiped away the tear and smiled. "Yeah. I think I am."

"What is it?"

Nisa wrapped her arms around Emmie's shoulders. "I think I connected with Dad."

"Nisa, that's wonderful!"

"Yeah, it is." She clung tighter. "I think he was telling me that everything will be okay."

The walk to Cole's hauler took longer than Nisa had expected. She kept getting stopped by people who'd known her dad. She felt better knowing that he'd been among family and friends when he'd been taken. Nisa quirked her lip at the memory.

Dad had made her stay home that day in a half-hearted attempt to punish her, because she hadn't finished all of her homework. Now, as an adult, she realized he'd done her a huge favor. She hadn't been there when her father hit the wall.

Cole's brawny arms wrapped Nisa in a tight hug when she and Emmie finally entered the hauler. When he released her, he asked, "Where have you been?"

"We ended up talking to some of Dad's friends along the way," she said.

Cole chuckled. "I can't say I'm surprised."

"Fifteen minutes, Cole."

Nisa turned, her eyes meeting those of her brother's crew chief. "Hi, Zeke."

"Nisa." The older man hugged her. "How're you holdin' up, honey?"

"Much better than I was this morning." She smiled, and caught Cole's questioning glance as Zeke released her.

"Did Ty come to see you?" Cole asked.

As much as she tried, she couldn't find any animosity toward his opponent in his voice. "He did," she admitted. "But that's not why I'm better." She hesitated to explain what she felt in case the two men watching her thought she was crazy.

"What is it?" Cole finally asked.

"I – I think I felt Dad's hand on my shoulder."

"Fifteen minutes." Zeke rolled his eyes as he left. Clearly he was a non-believer.

Cole didn't back down. "When?"

"On the way here," Nisa said. "I felt something heavy on my shoulder, but when I looked there was nothing there."

Cole grinned. *Oooooo-kaaay.* Not the reaction she was expecting.

"I'm glad you felt it," he said at last, hugging her tight. "I did, too, the first time I came back here to race. He's here, Nisa. Watching over us; keeping us both safe." He kissed the top of her head. "He's the reason I keep racing." He kept his hands on her biceps as he met her gaze.

Nisa shivered as she looked into her father's eyes.

"This place is awesome," Emmie exclaimed. "It's got everything."

"Well, it's not much, but it's home away from home." Cole let Nisa go and leaned against the wall of cabinets and drawers, highlighting some of the lesser-known features.

Seeing the inside of the sophisticated transporter through Emmie's eyes gave Nisa a whole new appreciation for how impressive it was. There were enough spare parts on board to build a whole new car, minus the engine and chassis. Though a spare motor was ready to go, in case Cole lost one before the race. Two cars were stored in the overhead compartment via a hydraulic lift gate, which doubled as a cover. The front of the hauler was a conference room with state-of-the-art electronics. An outsider would think they ran the space program.

It was a far cry from the oversized enclosed Featherlite Dad used to pull behind a heavy-duty pick-up truck. Nisa put her arm around Cole's waist as he put his around her shoulder.

He grinned. "Walk me out?"

Chapter 8

Nisa couldn't hold back her tears during the pre-race festivities. She wasn't the only one still grieving, she noticed, scanning the stands. Many of the fans dabbed their eyes during the video highlighting her dad's career on the Jumbotron.

She laughed during the clip of him hoisting her onto his shoulders in Victory Lane as they were both soaked with sports drinks and sodas. She'd been too young to remember it, but reliving that moment on this night would always be a cherished memory in her heart.

Cole gave a speech from the platform attached to the semi-truck parked along the front stretch. Nisa stood next to him, his arm around her, his hand resting on her right shoulder.

Suddenly she felt it again. That same presence from earlier, this time pressing Cole's arm into her neck and even heavier pressure on her left shoulder. Tears again filling her eyes, she glanced at Cole. His glistened, and she knew he felt it, too. She leaned her head against his arm. Warmth, like solid flesh and bone, seeped into her cheek. Her tears spilled over.

Cole was right.

Dad was here. With his children.

Enjoying this moment.

****

Three more minutes of silence. The calm before the storm.

The invocation had been given, the National Anthem sung.

Two more minutes.

The fly-by, courtesy of a fighter jet squadron, was complete, the pilots en route back to their base.

The drivers strapped into their cars.

One more minute. Nisa's already frayed nerves unraveled even more.

"Drivers! Start! Your! Engines!"

Kaaaaaaa-whoooomph!

The ground beneath her feet shook as forty high-powered stock cars roared to life all at the same time. The smell of high-octane fuel saturated the humid air.

Anticipation hung heavy.

Electricity crackled through the stands. Nisa climbed on top of the four-hundred-pound rolling toolbox, called the war wagon, set up behind Cole's pit stall. She and Emmie both wore headsets so they could hear every conversation between Zeke, Cole, and his spotter Will during the race, though they were unable to talk to them.

The drivers finally pulled off of pit road and lined up two-by-two. Pace cars paraded the racecars in two packs, helping the drivers set their pit road speeds.

The drivers swerved back and forth on the parade laps, keeping their tires free of the dust and debris that constantly blew across the track. They were nowhere near full race speed, but they were still going faster than cars on the highway.

Two laps to green.

The second pace car turned onto pit road, and the back half of the field caught up with the front. The official in the tower above the start/finish line held the green flag closed in his hand as he waved the field by.

One lap to green.

The lead pace car driver turned off the flashing lights.

The pack of forty cars drove off the back-straight into turn three. The pace car pulled onto pit lane. The official in the flag-stand held the drivers back, then unfurled the green to start the race. The drivers accelerated between turn four and the starting line.

Though she wore the headset and ear plugs, Nisa had to cover her ears from the roar of the unmuffled engines. The wind kicked up dust as the cars zoomed past.

Ty and Cole were side-by-side into turns one and two. Cole had the preferred groove, and maintained the advantage into turn three. Ty tucked in behind Cole coming off the banking in turn four.

Nisa sat on the edge of her seat for the first fifty of the four-hundred-lap race, then finally settled into the padded metal folding chair. Cole and Ty got separated about thirty laps in, with Ty getting shuffled back to hover between seventh and tenth place. Cole was still in command. The blistering pace he'd set early in the first run had him catching the tail end of the field within forty laps.

"She feels heavy in front," Cole said across the radio at lap sixty.

"Copy that," Zeke replied. "We'll make an air pressure adjustment on the first pit stop."

"How many laps?"

"No cautions, green-flag stops will start in about fifteen laps."

"Ten-four."

The radio fell silent. Nisa felt a tap on her shoulder, and she turned to her friend.

"What's happening?" Emmie shouted.

"Cole's starting to push." Nisa pointed to her brother's car as he drove into turn one. "See how the car fights to roll into the corner?"

Emmie nodded. Cole came dangerously close to the wall off the banking in turn two.

"That's a push," Nisa said. "The car has too much front grip and doesn't want to turn."

"What will they do?"

"Probably take some air out of the left front tire before they put it on the car."

Emmie nodded, and both girls turned back to the action. It wasn't a matter of *if* a caution came out, but *when*. Six hundred miles was a long race. Anything could, and usually did, happen.

Grease, burning rubber and the acrid stench of tire smoke joined the smell of exhaust. As the race transitioned from daylight to darkness around lap one-fifty, Nisa felt a prickling sensation along the back of her neck. She shifted in her seat, trying to shake it off. She found her binoculars trained as much on Ty's car as they were on her brother, though she didn't switch over to Ty's radio frequency.

He was still mired in fourteenth place. Cole had started on the inside pole position, and hadn't relinquished the lead since.

Seventy laps later that prickling sensation returned. Like something was going to happen. Cole lost the lead after the first round of green-flag stops, but regained it twenty laps later. His pace was still record-setting.

Ten laps later the screech of metal and the crunch of a hard hit had Nisa whipping around toward the backstretch. She relaxed when she saw that it was neither Cole nor Ty. The safety crews quickly cleaned up the mess, and racing resumed after another ten laps.

The first accident started a chain reaction. Ten more cars wrecked over the next ninety laps, none of them serious. Mainly fender-benders knocking cars into the wall or each other. Nisa smiled. *Cautions breed cautions.* For the most part, the top contenders ran a smart race. Everyone had managed to keep their heads out of their asses.

Her smile faded around lap two-eighty as she saw her brother mired about mid-pack after a bad stop. Cole was pissed. The air gun jammed for the rear tire changer, and he lost positions while the team swapped it out. Broken equipment during the race was one of those variables the team had planned for but prayed never happened.

With about a hundred laps left, Cole retook the lead and Ty finally got the right adjustments made to his car. They stayed nose-to-tail in the top two spots for another fifteen laps, until they each made their last scheduled stop of the night. Cole got his lead back once pit stops cycled through, Ty right on his heels.

The prickling sensation was back. Stronger. Nisa shifted in her seat, but couldn't dispel the feeling.

Cole and Ty dove hard into turn three again, mere inches separating their cars. Nisa could span her hand and touch both fenders at the same time.

"Status check," Zeke said to Cole across the radio.

"Car's good," Cole replied a moment later.

Nisa kept her gaze trained on his car as it sailed around the banking in turn one.

"Crash in turn four," Will said a couple laps later. "Go low."

"Copy." Cole dove to the bottom of the track.

"Lower, Cole." The radio crackled. "They're washing up the track."

"I see it." Cole dropped to the apron and tore into the huge cloud of white smoke.

Nisa held her breath.

He emerged a second later.

At the same time Ty plunged into the plume. He, too, appeared on the other side. Both cars were unscathed. Nisa let out a shaky sigh of relief.

"Woohoo!" Zeke yelled. "That's gonna make the highlight reels!"

Cole laughed. "Copy that!"

"What do you say we bring this baby home?"

"Ten-four," Cole agreed.

Nisa laughed with her brother. Emmie grinned next to her. Cole and Ty stayed P1 and P2 for the next twenty laps, but the P3 driver closed the gap. That sick feeling churned in the pit of Nisa's stomach, and she couldn't sit still. Getting to her feet, she paced the top of the pit box. Twenty seconds later, the car owner asked her to sit back down because the space was so limited. She complied, but her legs refused to remain still as her foot bounced against the diamond-stamped steel deck.

Ty drove hard into turn three with seventy to go, but the guy behind him was already there. Sparks flew. Tire smoke puffed. The crunch of metal was unmistakable. The third-place car had knocked Ty out of the way. The acrid stench of burnt rubber infiltrated the air and clogged Nisa's lungs. She stared as Ty careened up the track in Turn Three and hit the wall. Hard.

All of a sudden she was ten years old again, watching her father hit that same spot. Fear clogged her throat as his car rolled to a stop on the apron between turns three and four. Whisking off her headset, Nisa scurried down the ladder. When her feet hit the ground, she sprinted to the infield care center.

Cole was already out of turn two and heading for the backstretch when the caution flew.

****

Ty was pissed. What the hell was Oliver thinking, going after him like that? He threw the steering wheel onto the dash with more force than necessary. His gloves met the same fate. Then he remembered to lower the window net to let the safety crews know he was okay. He also had an in-car camera, so he wasn't too worried about anyone thinking he was hurt.

The most damage was done to his ego.

"Everything all right, Mr. Patterson?"

Ty looked at the guy from the safety crew and nodded. "I'm fine."

He removed his helmet and disengaged the safety harness before emerging from the car and examining the damage. Smoke poured from the busted radiator and water spilled onto the asphalt. The nose had accordioned on impact, pushing the wheel stubs back toward the firewall at least three inches. The hood was unsalvageable. Both front tires were flat, and the right-front ball joints were junk. He walked to the waiting ambulance.

The ride to the care center was a little bumpy because the driver hit a couple patches of grass along the backstretch. The medic asked him questions. Ty dutifully refrained from rolling his eyes and kept the sarcasm from his voice.

When he got to the infield care center they took him into a curtained-off cubicle. The doctor asked him more questions. He cursed silently when the bastard shined a light into his eyes with no warning. He flinched.

The doc had the audacity to chuckle. "You're fine, Mr. Patterson. But you'll probably be sore in the morning."

"I don't doubt that," Ty said. "Thanks, doc." He tied the sleeves of his fire suit around his waist and walked to the lobby. He stopped dead in his tracks. Nisa leaned against the wall. Her eyes were red and puffy.

"Nisa?" He walked over and laid his hand on her arm. Tears stained her cheeks when she looked at him. "What are you doin' here, sweetheart?"

She sniffled. "I – I had to make sure you were okay."

She's crying over me. The thought warmed his heart. He went over to her and wiped away one of the trails. "I'm fine," he assured. "It looked worse than it was."

Nisa launched herself at him. He caught her in his arms, the impact jarring against his battered body. "Oomph! Easy, darlin'."

She wrapped her arms around his neck and held tight. He breathed in her scent. The grit and grease from the track, and something pure Nisa. He'd never get tired of her. "Are you okay, honey?"

"I thought I'd lost you," she said against his skin. "It was like watching my father all over again."

Of course watching him hit the wall reminded her of her father. Even as he comforted her, holding her close sent his body into a tailspin. He had to let her go, otherwise the cameras would get one helluva show. "I'm right here, darlin'. Alive and well." And he still had a job to do.

"I needed to make sure." Her voice was muffled against his throat.

"I want to talk to you more, but I don't have time right now." Ty tried prying her arms from around his neck. "I need to talk to the reporters."

She held tighter.

"Nisa," he said with more force. "Unless you want to announce to the world that we're a couple, you need to let me go."

She pulled back, startled.

He lightly kissed her on the mouth. "We'll talk later," he promised. "Wait a few minutes before leaving."

She nodded, finally releasing her hold on his neck. He calmed his over-excited body as he exited the medical center. He answered all of the reporters' questions patiently, again refraining from rolling his eyes. The first thing he learned when he entered the world of professional sports was that the cameras saw everything.

He didn't look back to see if Nisa had honored his request. Instinctively he knew she had.

Chapter 9

Nisa made her way back to Cole's pit box at a more sedate pace than she'd left it. The race had resumed, and she donned the noise-reducing headset. Emmie gave her a weird look as she sat back down, but she waved it off.

"'Bout damn time!" Emmie shouted over the noise. "How's Ty?"

Nisa gave her friend the thumbs-up. She wanted to talk more about him, but the engine roar made it nearly impossible. "Later!" she shouted back. "What did I miss?"

"Dropped to tenth four laps ago," Emmie replied.

Cole had raced back into fifth place, according to the scoring pylon between turns one and two. Nisa followed his car for a few laps before scanning the rest of the field. Seven cars raced in a tight pack a quarter lap behind Cole. Nisa held her breath for a heartbeat, watching to see how they sorted themselves out. One car drove hard into the outside lane, right against the wall. It looked like he had the power to muscle by them on the high side as they all sailed into turn three, four-wide.

Nisa's heart pounded as the action unfolded in slow-motion. *Someone's gotta give.* Adrenaline surged through her. At the entrance of turn three the car along the apron drifted high toward the middle of the track, directly into the car on his right. The car in the middle groove backed off the gas a split second before almost being sandwiched between the cars on either side.

The two cars on the low side also backed off to keep from wrecking each other, opening the door for the car on the outside to drive right by them coming off the dogleg out of turn four.

Gutsy move. Nisa finally released the breath she'd been holding.

"Whoa!" Emmie hooted. "That was awesome!"

Nisa nodded, grinning. She'd forgotten how exciting racing could be. She looked at the pylon again. Cole had moved up to fourth with thirty-five laps to go.

"We're not gonna make it, Cole," Zeke said over the radio. "We're ten laps short."

"Can anyone make it from here?" Cole responded.

"Uh … looks like the sixty-eight might, but it's gonna be awful close. He's the only one gonna try."

"When should I pit?"

"Two laps." Zeke made the call. "Gas 'n go only. Don't flat-spot the tires."

"Ten-four." The radio fell silent.

Emmie tapped Nisa's shoulder. "What's the call?"

"Cole can't make it to the end without running out of gas," Nisa replied. "He's gonna pit next time by."

Emmie nodded.

Despite having been away from the sport for twenty years, Nisa was surprised at how quickly she'd picked up the lingo again.

Cole's team had stayed on top of the changing track conditions all night. He was about to take third place when he drove to the inside and slowed on the backstretch, ready to pit.

"Six seconds of fuel," Zeke instructed.

"Five … four … three … two … pit," Will said over the radio, guiding Cole into his stall.

Zeke counted out the fuel and Cole glided smoothly out of his pit.

"Why didn't he take tires?" Emmie asked.

"Didn't need 'em," Nisa said. "His tires haven't fallen off as much as the other drivers."

Emmie leaned closer. "What does that mean?"

"New tires have better grip and more speed," Nisa explained over the roar of the pack. "Once they build up heat, they lose speed and grip."

"How much speed?" Emmie shouted.

"Depends on the driver." Nisa pointed to a pack of eight cars coming off Turn Two. "The harder they race, the faster they lose grip." She grabbed a spare laptop from the docking station next to Zeke and opened a spreadsheet document from last week's race, explaining the difference in lap times. She amazed herself with the ability to recognize the gradual tire wear.

"Gotcha." Emmie sat back in her seat.

Nisa focused back on the track.

"You're running about three seconds ahead of the leader," Zeke said to Cole.

"When do they have to pit?"

"Within the next ten laps. Do what you can."

"Ten-four."

The pylon displayed forty laps left. One-by-one, the top drivers came in for fuel. A couple gambled and took on fresh right-side rubber. Cole steadily moved back up to second place, but he was still a half lap behind the leader with ten to go. His closest competitor was the length of the straightaway behind him.

Nisa watched the sixty-eight car from the edge of her seat as the laps dwindled. With five to go, Cole was still about four car-lengths behind the leader, but he was gaining fast. The sixty-eight slowed considerably but still maintained point.

Two laps left. On a surge of raw power Cole shot up behind the leader, whose car nearly broke loose off the banking in turn two.

"YES!" Nisa leapt to her feet and pumped her fists into the air. The leader hiccupped down the backstretch coming to the white flag, the rear end of his car fishtailing. "Go Cole!"

"What happened?" Emmie shouted, also jumping to her feet.

Nisa pointed as Cole overtook the leader. The sixty-eight wiggled back and forth in the center of the corner. "Out of gas!"

Cole took the white flag. Emmie jumped up and down on top of the pit box. Nisa stayed rooted to her spot as she watched Cole maneuver his sixty-three car smoothly through lapped traffic down the backstretch one more time. The sixty-eight faded into the pack as his fuel evaporated. The second-place car was still several seconds behind him. Nisa knew the race wasn't over until the checkers. Anything could happen in the next lap.

"It's yours buddy," Zeke said over the radio as Cole took the checkered flag. "Congratulations!"

"Great job, boys!" Cole cheered to his crew.

Nisa finally jumped up and down in celebration. She hugged Emmie tight, their hard plastic headsets clashing over their ears.

"Let's go to Victory Lane!" Emmie shouted.

Nisa nodded, grinning as she removed her headset. They scampered down the ladder and headed in that direction. Huge plumes of white smoke billowed out from beneath Cole's car as he spun burnouts on the front stretch and the team high-fived on pit road. She paused, watching as Cole caught the checkered flag from the official in the flag-stand and drove around the track, waving the flag out the window in salute to the fans. Fireworks exploded from high above the grandstands, showers of color glittering in the night sky.

Nisa and Emmie joined Zeke and the rest of the crew on the platform as Cole drove into Victory Lane. The camera crews swarmed as confetti rained down on them.

A hand touched Nisa's shoulder, and she turned.

Cole's PR director handed her a towel and a baseball cap in his primary sponsor colors. "Here." He thrust her toward the car.

She stumbled, but caught herself and went over to Cole, leaning into the window. "Here you go."

"Thanks, sis." He took the towel and wiped the sweat off his face, then shoved his cap over a serious case of helmet hair.

Nisa giggled as she felt another tap on her shoulder. She looked up, seeing the network television cameras. "I think it's time to come out," she told her brother. They shared a smile, then she stepped back to let him enjoy the spotlight.

He put his hands on hers. "Where do you think you're going?"

Confusion knitted her brow. "What?"

"Find your pretty smile, sis, because you're staying right here." Cole emerged from the car a moment later, to the cheer of the crowd and more confetti. He stood on the window ledge and pumped his fists in the air, howling in victory. He grabbed one of the sports drink bottles and sprayed it everywhere. The team fought back with champagne.

I'm glad I'm not wearing white, Nisa thought as red and gold liquid rained down on her.

It only took seconds for her to get completely drenched from head to toe. She brushed her wet hair away from her face and looked at Emmie, who grinned from ear to ear.

Cole leapt from the car and the reporters crowded in. Nisa only half-listened to the interview, even though her brother held her next to him.

"Daddy was definitely watching over me today." Cole wrapped up the interview.

"Hollywood couldn't have written a better script," the reporter said into the camera. "Congratulations again, Cole."

More champagne drenched the crew as Nisa dashed out of the spray.

"So that's what it feels like!" Emmie shouted over the noise.

"What?" Nisa shouted back.

Emmie grinned. "The champagne shower!"

Nisa nodded, smiling back.

Cole's PR director handed her a towel. "Cole wants you in the pictures."

Nisa panicked as she wiped the sticky-sweet liquid from her face and wrung out her hair, then raked the damp tresses into a ponytail and covered her head with a baseball cap. She grabbed Emmie's hand and dragged her along to the podium.

Someone gave each of the crew guys a bag of hats for the "hat dance," where they changed hats literally after every photograph. Cole knelt next to the trophy. Nisa was on his left side. Emmie wanted to hide in the back, but Nisa wouldn't let her. "Hey, if I have to be front and center, so do you." She brushed a strand of hair from her eyes. "It'll probably be a once-in-a-lifetime experience."

After a moment of grumbling and griping, Emmie knelt next to her on the platform. By the time the final picture was taken, Nisa felt like her face was going to fall off from smiling and her wet clothes were glued to her skin.

Zeke barked orders to the crew as Nisa, Cole and Emmie headed back to Cole's motor coach. He stopped as they passed Ty's hauler, whose team was in the process of loading the wrecked racecar into the overhead storage compartment. That sick feeling churned in the pit of Nisa's stomach again.

"Hey, Pete," Cole said to Ty's crew chief. "Is Ty around?"

"Congrats." Pete shook Cole's hand. "You missed him. He left about twenty minutes ago."

Cole nodded as Nisa's heart sank. They resumed their path to his motor coach, and he pulled her into his arms. "I'm sorry, Nisa."

"I am too," she said against his neck.

"See you at breakfast." He kissed her cheek and headed for the private parking lot.

Nisa and Emmie went into the coach and locked up for the night.

After a quick shower Nisa changed and climbed between the sheets.

****

The acrid stench of burning rubber sears her nostrils as smoke clogs her lungs. She coughs, but it only gets worse. The hard crunch of metal against concrete rents the air and a fireball blasts through the fence toward the fans.

The smoke clears enough for her to see the number painted on the door panel. Ty.

Her heart pounds.

The safety crew looks like ants crawling around the car. Time slows as the driver is finally extricated from the wreck. What's left of the car is loaded onto a roll-back truck.

Someone covers it with a black tarp.

She screams.

****

Nisa jolted awake, her body drenched in sweat. She pushed damp hair out of her eyes, kicking off the blankets.

She went to the galley kitchen and filled a glass with water. The cold liquid soothed her parched throat as she drank deeply.

"Are you okay?"

Nisa jumped at the sound of her friend's voice.

"I heard you scream." Emmie leaned against the counter. "Was it a nightmare?"

Nisa nodded, taking another drink.

Emmie hugged her. "Want to talk about it?"

Nisa shook her head, then changed her mind. "Sure." She refilled her glass and strode to the living room.

"I'll meet you in the living room." Emmie filled her own glass as Nisa settled on the sofa opposite where Emmie had been sleeping.

Emmie snuggled into her blankets. "What happened?"

"I dreamt that Ty had died after hitting the wall," Nisa blurted.

Emmie said nothing for a moment, then let out a low whistle. "That's messed up."

"I know." Nisa sipped her water. "He hit the wall like he did tonight, except the car burst into flames and killed him."

Emmie rose and sat next to Nisa, hugging her. "I'm sorry, hon."

Nisa took comfort in her friend's embrace.

"Is that how your dad died?" Emmie asked a minute later.

Nisa hiccupped, her eyes brimming with tears. "Yeah, except there was no fire."

"Why do you think your dream included fire?"

Nisa shrugged. "My wild imagination, I guess." She wiped a tear from her eye.

"A driver's worst fear," Emmie confirmed.

Nisa pushed off the sofa and paced the length of the aisle, shoving her fingers through her hair. "I never should've come back."

Emmie stared back at her as if she'd suddenly grown an extra head and a few more limbs. "But you'd never have met him."

"That's why!" Nisa spun around in frustration, marching a few steps toward the cockpit.

"I thought you loved him?"

Emmie's quiet words tore Nisa apart and stopped her in her tracks. "I think I might." She kept her voice equally soft. "That's why this is so hard." She plopped back on the sofa next to Emmie. "I can't go through that again. I'm not strong enough."

"Nisa, you're one of the strongest people I know." Emmie hugged her again. "I think that coming back here has helped you heal that place inside of you. If it hadn't you wouldn't have been able to fall for a guy who shared your dad's profession."

Nisa considered Emmie's words. "Why would he leave without saying anything to me?"

"I don't know, hon. But I'm sure he had a good reason." Emmie yawned. "Think you can get some sleep? We have a flight to catch tomorrow."

Nisa looked at the glowing numbers on the microwave. Three in the morning. They were meeting Cole at the Speedway Club for breakfast in a few hours, before catching their late-morning flight back to La Crosse. She nodded, showing more confidence than she felt. "I'll see you in the morning."

Nisa went back to the bedroom and slid beneath the blankets. Hot tears scalded her eyes and dripped onto the pillow beneath her head. She sniffed, valiantly trying to keep a stiff upper lip as emotions overwhelmed her. She quickly lost the battle and cried herself to sleep.

Chapter 10

Ty rose at seven and went for his run on Monday morning, feeling every one of the hits he'd taken on the track the night before. He kept to the lesser-known trails around Lake Norman, his muscles loosening with each stride. He replayed the wreck in his mind while he ran, wondering if there was anything he could've done differently and if he could carry something over to the next week's race in Dover.

The post-race briefing with his crew after the race had been short and to the point, watching replays of the wreck, then discussing the events leading up to when he hit the wall. He'd regretted having to leave the track without talking to Nisa, but he couldn't have avoided it if he'd tried. His PA had given him a ride to the track, and they'd had to leave once his interviews were over.

After his run he showered and dressed, hoping to get to the track before Nisa left. When he got to the infield, he drove to the private lot and knocked on the door to Cole's RV. His heart sank when she didn't answer.

"Mornin', Ty."

He turned, smiling at the security guard.

"Lookin' for Cole?" the guard asked.

"Yeah," Ty lied, nodding.

"I saw him head up to the Speedway Club about thirty minutes ago."

"Thanks." He tipped his hat and headed toward the grandstands. It didn't take him long to spot Cole in the restaurant. He strode toward the table, relieved that Nisa was still with him. Cole saw him first, as she was sitting with her back to the door.

"Ty," Cole said, standing.

"Cole." Ty extended a hand to his fellow racer, and winced when Cole squeezed a little too hard. "Can I talk to your sister for a few minutes?"

Cole sat back down. "That's up to her."

"Nisa?" Ty asked, suddenly afraid she'd say no.

After a long moment she finally looked at him. Her eyes were tinged with pink, her expression clouded by sadness. He couldn't help himself and pulled her into his arms, holding her tight. "I'm so sorry, sweetheart."

She stayed in his arms, but he was worried he'd blown his shot with her. "What's wrong?"

Her arms snaked around his neck, but she still didn't say anything. He guided her to the cloakroom and kissed her, gently trying to coax a response. As he started drawing away, her lips moved beneath his and her tongue darted out. Sweet elation filled his senses and his heart overflowed with emotion. He parted her lips with his tongue and delved deeper. When he finally released her, they were both breathing hard, and his heart threatened to burst from his chest. He cupped her face in his hands. "What's the matter, Nisa?"

"You – I –" She broke off. "I can't do this again."

He furrowed his brow. "Do what again?"

"Last night … it was my dad all over again." She sniffled. "I never should've come back." She kissed him again. It was bittersweet. "I'm sorry, Ty. Take care of yourself, okay?"

"Wait." He caught her arm as she turned to leave. "What does that mean?"

"I'm not strong enough, Ty." Her eyes filled with tears.

His insides clenched with fear. "Are you saying good-bye?"

She nodded.

"Without giving us a chance?" He couldn't believe she was walking away. "What about last night?"

"What about it?" Her eyes sparkled with tears. "You said you'd look for me after the race, but then you left."

"I regret that, but it couldn't be helped." He shoved his fingers through his hair in frustration. "I had something I needed to take care of."

"It doesn't matter anymore." Her expression changed. "I can't go through that again."

"You've said that three times now," he countered. "What are you talking about?"

"You're kidding, right?" Her tone was incredulous. "Ty, you hit the wall ten feet from where my dad was killed. How do you think that makes me feel?"

His heart clenched again. Ty hadn't given it much thought after last night. Or how difficult watching him crash had been for her. Though the way she'd raced to the medical center afterward should've given him a clue.

"I'm sorry, Ty, I –" she broke off. "I can't." She left the cloakroom and headed back to the table.

"Is everything all right, Mr. Patterson?"

Ty turned to the manager. "Yes," he lied. "Everything's fine."

With one last look at Nisa's back as she sat down in her chair, he left the restaurant, vowing to not let her go without a fight.

****

Nisa ignored Cole's questioning glance as she picked up her fork again, but her appetite fled. Emmie ran her hand over Nisa's back. Nisa closed her eyes, fighting tears.

"Will you be okay?" Cole asked.

Nisa nodded, not trusting her voice. She ate a bite of her omelet, but couldn't force it past the lump clogging her throat. Setting her fork on the table, she discreetly spit the food into her napkin. She didn't say a word while Cole and Emmie finished their breakfast.

The waitress cleared their table as Cole took care of the bill. They'd ended up getting a commercial flight home, and twenty minutes later they were on their way to the Charlotte-Douglas Airport. Cole accompanied them to the security checkpoint, giving her a big hug.

"I'll be back up there in a few weeks when we race at Michigan," he said against her hair. "I'll clear some time for you."

"Okay." Her voice was a broken whisper.

He let her go. Nisa and Emmie went through airport security and found their gate.

"Will you be okay?" Emmie asked.

"Yes. No." Nisa sighed. "I don't know." Her heart was hurting, and she didn't know how to make it stop.

The flight back was uneventful, and Nisa had too much time to think. They touched down smoothly at O'Hare airport a few hours later and caught the puddle-jumper back to La Crosse.

"Why couldn't we have flown back on the Gulfstream?" Emmie complained as they waited for the luggage carousel at the La Crosse Municipal Airport.

"What difference does it make?" Nisa asked.

"Well, none really," Emmie hedged, "but the Gulfstream was more comfortable."

Nisa agreed, but she kept quiet. After taking Emmie home, she returned to her house on the north side of Onalaska. After tossing her weekend bag on the floor of her bedroom, she flopped on the bed and burst into tears.

Chapter 11

Tuesday morning, Nisa was sketching a new design in her notebook when a sharp knock caught her attention. A slender brunette poked her head into the cupboard-sized office.

"How did your weekend go?" Felicia asked.

Nisa turned to her boss. "Good. Cole won the race."

Felicia sat in the chair across from her. "That's good." She paused. "I can't imagine how hard it was for you, going back to the same track where –"

"It was." Nisa cut her off. "But I was able to make peace with what happened." *For the most part.*

"I'm glad." Felicia peered at the notebook. "Something new?"

"Yeah." She showed the design.

"NASCAR championship ring," Felicia said. "Very nice, but we can't sell it here."

Nisa closed the notebook. "Just an idea I'm toying with."

"How are the engagement designs coming?"

"Finished this morning." Nisa flipped to the page and passed it over.

Felicia perused the renderings, saying nothing for a few moments. She finally handed the notebook back to Nisa. "How soon will they be ready for presentation?"

"Presentation?" she squeaked, a bit stunned.

"To the board." Felicia looked amused. "Your designs, your pitch."

"When is the next meeting?"

"I believe it's next week."

Nisa's heart sank. "I don't know if I can have a sales pitch ready by then."

"I know your collection will be approved," Felicia said. "They won't want to wait on production when they do. As always, your creations are stunning."

Nisa nodded. "Can I get some help?"

"Sure." Felicia strode to the door. "I expect a rough draft by this Friday."

"Thanks." Nisa's hand trembled as she picked up her pencil. When she'd gone into jewelry design, she hadn't realized she'd have to create her own sales pitches.

The chairman of the board at Klausen Gems was old-fashioned, insisting all employees know all facets of the small, family-run organization. Though he employed a modest marketing team, Viktor Klausen insisted that his designers also promoted their own collections.

Nisa had had two collections approved and put into the sales showcases already, so she knew what she was doing. But that still didn't make giving sales pitches any easier. And she still didn't have enough confidence in her own marketing abilities to go at this one by herself. She picked up the phone.

"Bryan Newton," the warm tenor voice resonated on the other end of the connection.

Nisa smiled. "Hey, Fig."

"Hey, Twig." Bryan said. "What's up?"

"I need your help."

"Of course you do." He chuckled. "What is it this time?"

She tapped the eraser of her pencil against the paper. "Felicia wants me to make a presentation to the board."

"And you called me?" He sounded surprised.

"You're head of marketing, aren't you?" she teased.

"My office, fifteen minutes," he said. "Bring your sketches."

"Aye, aye, sir."

"Smartass." His tone was deadpan.

She stuck out her tongue at the receiver. "Takes one to know one."

****

Three weeks passed since Charlotte, and Nisa's heart still remained heavy. Ty had called a couple times, but she hadn't answered. Returning to the track had opened the floodgates on memories that now refuse to be suppressed, and she needed more time to process her emotions. She still hadn't figured out what she was going to do about Ty, and she didn't think it fair to give him false hope.

She lifted her head, the commotion from the sales floor carrying down the hall to her office. She wheeled her chair from behind her desk and went to the door. "What's going on?" she asked Janessa, who'd rushed into her office.

"One of the hottest athletes in the world is in our store! The customers are flocking to him for autographs." Janessa smirked. "Mainly women."

"Athlete?" Nisa muttered as she headed for the showroom, half-expecting to see Cole. He'd said he was coming into town that evening. *Maybe he came in early.*

When Nisa approached the front, she gasped. Ty was signing a woman's t-shirt. *What's he doing here? Where's Cole?* She was about to go to him when Viktor Klausen appeared and shook Ty's hand, introducing himself as the owner.

"I need some jewelry," she heard Ty say as they disappeared into a private viewing room.

Jewelry? She was about to follow when her boss stopped her.

"You're as pale as a sheet," Felicia said. "What's wrong?"

"I – I'm not – I don't know," Nisa stuttered. "I'm curious why Ty Patterson is in La Crosse, shopping for jewelry, of all things." Though she had a sneaking suspicion he'd come to see her.

Felicia looked perplexed. "You know Ty?"

Nisa looked around, making sure they were alone. "We met at the racetrack.

"With your brother."

"I met Ty at a party on Thursday night, but I didn't know who he was until Sunday morning." Nisa sighed. Not the whole truth, but it would suffice for now.

"He's your brother's biggest rival." Felicia quirked her brow. "How did you not know who he was?"

"I haven't followed NASCAR since my dad –" she broke off. "Anyway, we danced at the party, and had lunch on Friday. But I didn't know his full name until my dad's memorial on Sunday morning."

"So why is he here?"

"Good question." Nisa looked at her watch, an intricate design she'd created to resemble vines encircling her wrist, the mother-of-pearl face gleaming opalescent beneath the fluorescent lights. "I'm going to lunch."

Felicia nodded. "I'll see you when you get back."

Nisa returned to her office. Switching her phone to voice mail, she grabbed her purse and strode to the employee entrance. She didn't want to stick around in case he was buying a gift for another woman. But if it was for her, she didn't want him presenting it to her in front of her coworkers. She knew she was being cowardly, but she still hadn't resolved her issues with him being a racecar driver despite having made peace with her dad's death. In fact, she'd gained a whole new respect for Cole, and for the other drivers.

Nisa crossed the busy street at the light, heading for the Mexican restaurant. She kept her head down as she walked, not wanting to draw attention to herself. She made it to the restaurant and ordered her food, then she sat at one of the tables by the window facing the jewelry store.

She kept an eye on the front door as she ate, only relaxing when she saw Ty get into a sleek sapphire Mustang convertible and drive away.

She relaxed a little as she finished her lunch and returned to her office. Hoping that she wouldn't have to answer questions from her boss, she walked into her office, and was stuffing her purse into the bottom desk drawer when a voice that shouldn't be there was.

"You didn't think I'd let you get away that easy, did you?"

Nisa jumped as the sound of Ty's easy drawl came from the doorway. "Ty, what are you doing here?" It was the only coherent thought that popped into her head.

His lips twisted into a wry smile. "That should be obvious. I'm here to see you." He stepped into her office and closed the door. "Why haven't you called me back?"

"I'm sorry." The words sounded trite, even to her ears. "I've been putting a sales pitch together for my new collection, which has taken up all my spare time."

"And now?" He erased the short distance between them with a few strides. He took her face between his palms.

Nisa's knees threatened to buckle and her blood simmered in her veins as Ty's mouth closed in on hers. The brush of his lips against hers ignited an inferno within her. She slipped her fingers into his hair, finding anchor in the sensual onslaught as he deepened the kiss. Regardless of how she felt about his career, his kisses still made her blood fizz.

The last three weeks apart melted as if they'd never happened. Suddenly Nisa was back in the infield after he'd been released from the medical center. She tightened her hold on his hair and kissed him harder. Their mouths fused together and her breath burned in her lungs.

"Nisa, have you –" The office door burst open.

Nisa gasped and ripped her mouth from his, though the steel band of his arm kept her close.

"I'm sorry." Janessa smirked. "I didn't realize you had company."

"It's fine, Janessa. What did you need?" Nisa asked, recovering her equilibrium.

"Viktor wants to know if you've finished the sketches for your final designs," the older woman said.

"Tell him he'll have them by the end of the day."

"He'll hold you to that." Janessa sashayed back into the hallway.

Nisa turned back to Ty, smiling in apology. "I'd better get back to work."

"Of course." Ty reluctantly let her go. "What designs?"

Nisa crossed to her drafting table and lifted the cover on the sketch pad.

"Oh, wow." He flipped through the pages. "You did all these?"

Nisa nodded. "They've been approved by the board. I'm polishing them up for production."

"Gorgeous." He closed the cover on the pad. "Have dinner with me tonight."

She furrowed her brow. "Shouldn't you be getting ready for the Michigan?"

"The first practice isn't until Friday morning," he said. "I cleared my schedule for tonight. Please come out with me."

She remembered his earlier words to Viktor. "What about your girlfriend?" The words slipped out before she could stop them.

Ty frowned. "I don't have a girlfriend."

"Then why –" she broke off when a strange glint appeared in his cerulean eyes.

"If you want the answer to that question," he said evenly, "meet me at The Waterfront at six." His finger trailed along the V-neck of her blouse from her shoulder to above the shadowed valley of her cleavage. "Come as you are."

He planted another quick, hard kiss on her mouth, then left her office.

Nisa stared at the door, her mind complete mush, and her fingers over her tingling lips.

"What was Ty Patterson doing here?" Felicia popped her head into the doorway. "Where can I get one of those hunks for myself?"

"Apparently ordering jewelry." Nisa shrugged. "I heard him talking to Viktor earlier. I'm sorry, Felicia, did you want something?"

"I've come for the designs on the Eternal Embrace collection. Viktor wants them pronto."

Nisa squeezed the bridge of her nose between her fingers. "Can I have thirty minutes?"

"Let me see where you're at."

Nisa grabbed the sketch pad from the drafting table again and handed to her boss, who studied the designs.

"I love them the way they are," Felicia said at last. "I'm sure Viktor will, too. Excellent work, as always."

Heat scorched Nisa's face. "Thank you."

Felicia left with the designs as Nisa returned to her desk. She finished sketching a piece for her personal Valentine's Day collection ten minutes later when Felicia came back with her notebook.

"I'll let you know what Viktor says tomorrow." Felicia set the pad on the table and walked back over to the desk. "That's pretty," she said of the delicate heart-shaped filigree pendant studded with two-point rubies. "Is that for the Love's Kiss collection?"

"I'm hoping to put it under my own label," Nisa said.

"I can't guarantee that," Felicia hedged, "but I'll talk to Viktor and see what I can do."

****

The hostess greeted Nisa as she entered the restaurant. She spotted Ty right away, seated at a table overlooking the main channel of the Mississippi River as it ebbed and flowed past Riverside Park on its journey south.

Nisa had been able to put Ty's kiss out of her mind while she focused on her job, but it was all she could think about as she'd gathered her purse and locked her office door. As she'd walked to her car, self-preservation had warred with curiosity. Curiosity won and she'd found herself walking the seven blocks to The Waterfront.

Nisa headed for his table, her heart pounding in her chest. "Hello, Ty."

"Nisa." He rose, helping her into the chair opposite his, placing a kiss on the exposed side of her neck. "Thank you for meeting me."

"You didn't leave me much choice." Her voice lacked heat. She wasn't even upset with him. She'd gotten used to him being aggressive with her.

He cleared his throat. "You look amazing."

"Thank you." The waitress filled her water glass. Nisa took a healthy sip to calm her nerves.

"I've missed you." He took her hand across the table. "Being at the track isn't the same without you."

Nisa looked out the window, saying nothing as she watched a leaf drifting helplessly along the swift current. She sympathized with the leaf, because that's how she felt whenever she was around Ty. She faced him again, their gazes locking across the table. The emotions in his green eyes stole her breath.

"Ty, I –" she stammered. "I've missed you too."

"I especially miss the way you launched into my arms when you thought I'd been hurt."

Heat flushed through her entire body, remembering that embrace, and the subsequent kiss that had left her wanting more. Which was why it hurt when he hadn't stayed after the race.

But he came back the next morning, her subconscious pointed out. *And he's here now. He cares.*

His thumb stroked across her knuckles, jolting Nisa from her thoughts. "I liked it too," she said quietly. "That's why this is so hard."

The waitress chose that moment to take their food orders. Ty took the liberty of ordering for both of them. She should've been annoyed, but he'd requested items she would've chosen anyway. She quirked her brow. "How did you know I'd like what you ordered?"

Twin slashes of color appeared across his high cheekbones. "I, um, I sort of asked Cole."

"You talked to my brother?" Nisa kept her voice neutral, but her heart raced as fast as his car.

"Please don't be mad," Ty pleaded. "I told him I wanted to see you again, away from the track."

Nisa took another sip of water. "What did he say?"

"That it was up to you." The corner of his mouth quirked up mirthlessly. "He told me about your dad, and why you moved up here instead of staying in Charlotte."

"I couldn't stay," she said.

"I know. And I don't blame you for leaving." Ty sipped his drink as he, too, looked out the window. "I can see why you moved here. La Crosse is beautiful."

"It reminds me a lot of Darlington," she replied. "They're both decent-sized cities with a small-town feel."

Ty set his glass on the beverage napkin and faced her again. "Would you consider moving back to North Carolina?"

The softly-asked question caught her by surprise. "I've been away so long that I haven't given it much thought." She shrugged. "I've spent twenty years here. I've built a quiet life away from the spotlight shining on Cole, and I'm not sure I want to return to it."

"You did well during the race," he pointed out.

She drained her glass. "That wasn't about me."

"What are you afraid of?" he asked softly.

The waitress appeared with their entrees, saving Nisa from having to answer as Ty steered the conversation into less-volatile channels. But his question stayed with her throughout dinner, undermining all of her concerns about a relationship with him.

They discovered similar tastes in music and movies, and they shared a love of classic American muscle cars. While Ty was a Mopar fan, Nisa loved Mustangs.

"I'm definitely a pony girl," she said, laughing at his expression. "Though my daddy had this 1970 Barracuda that was absolutely gorgeous." A bolt of melancholy flashed through her, and she gazed out the window again. Ever since she'd come home she'd been hit with occasional memories of her father.

Ty took her hand again. "What is it?"

She shook it off. "I was thinking of my dad again."

"You miss him." It wasn't a question.

She nodded. "I do."

"Want to talk about him?"

"No." she shook her head. "I'm okay. It's just …"

"What?" Ty asked.

Nisa sighed. "Every now and then something triggers a memory, and I miss him all over again."

"Does it happen often?" Ty winced after he spoke, bringing her hand to his lips. "I'm sorry. You don't have to tell me." He brushed a kiss across her knuckles.

"Thank you." Nisa opted to not answer the question, though a shiver snaked up her arm from his caress.

He furrowed his brow. "For what?"

"Understanding. Not pushing."

"Of course." He placed her hand flat on the table and covered it with his. "What would you like to do tonight?"

She looked up, surprised. "You don't have to get back?"

"I have the team jet on standby. I can leave early tomorrow morning." He snared her gaze with his. "That is, if you want me to stay."

Nisa couldn't look away if she'd tried. Heat seared through her from his direct look, his deep blue eyes as mesmerizing as they had been when he'd asked her to dance in Charlotte. She nodded, her head feeling like it moved without her knowledge or consent.

"I'd like to hear you say it." His voice was soft but intense. "So there's no confusion. No doubts."

She knew what he was asking. The waitress brought the check and cleared the table. Nisa waited until Ty had signed the slip and put his credit card back in his wallet before she said anything. "Yes, Ty. I'd like for you to stay."

He grew still. "Are you sure?"

"Yes, I'm sure." Nisa nodded. "Though I still have reservations about getting involved with a hotshot NASCAR driver." She flashed him a cheeky grin. "My small-town life might be too slow for him."

Ty returned her grin. "Then again, maybe not. I'm from Kingsport, remember?"

She covered his hand on the table with hers. "Let me show you why I love it here."

"How can I resist?"

Ty stayed in her rearview mirror on her way back to her house on the north side of Onalaska.

"Nice place," he said, following her from the kitchen to the dining room.

"Thank you." She dropped her purse onto the table. Her keys landed next to it. "It suits my needs, and the payments are cheap."

"When was that taken?" Ty pointed to a portrait on the wall above the flat-screen TV.

"Dover, about fifteen years ago. Make yourself comfortable. I'm going to change."

Nisa left him to study the photographs as she returned to her bedroom off the kitchen. She changed from her work garb into clothes more conducive to relaxed sightseeing, then grabbed an elastic hair tie from the basket in the bathroom and wrapped it around her long mahogany tresses as she stood next to him in the sitting room. He was still studying the portrait.

"Cole put me in his racecar for my sixteenth birthday." She interrupted his reverie.

"At Dover?" He sounded surprised.

She nodded. "I was only supposed to turn a few laps, but I ended up staying out for about twenty minutes of the first practice session."

Ty whistled. "I'm impressed."

"Especially for having never been behind the wheel of a racecar before." She grinned.

"Why did he keep you out there?"

"Apparently my lap times were consistently within the top three. I briefly held the fastest lap." Nisa smirked. "Until Mark Martin knocked me off of it."

His eyes held a curious light. "Why didn't you stay out the whole practice?"

"Blame the Intimidator." She shrugged. "Plus it was supposed to be Cole's hot-lap session, not mine."

"Serves you right for tanglin' with the Black Three." Ty laughed, admiration shining from his azure eyes. "What happened?"

"He came up on me a little too fast coming out of turn two. Took the air off my spoiler. I lost downforce off the deck lid and she started to lift." Nisa rubbed her arms. "I didn't have the experience to bring the car back around, and I hit the wall hard along the backstretch."

"Still, for a rookie, any rookie, to do what you did was incredible." Admiration shone in his eyes. And maybe a hint of jealousy? "Are you up for another ride?"

Nisa shook her head. "Sorry, champ. That was a one-shot deal."

His grin turned mischievous. "Are you sure I can't persuade you?"

She stood firm, crossing her arms over her chest. "Though it did give me a whole new appreciation for what Dad did. What Cole still needs to do to stay in peak condition at his age."

Ty chuckled. "He doesn't seem to be slowing down any time soon."

"No, he doesn't." Nisa smiled. "I think it's his experience that helps him compete even though he'll be fifty in September."

"I hope I can be half as competitive as he is when I reach his age."

"Right? I mean, how many other sports have athletes that are still as competitive as the guys half their age?" She said it as a throw away remark, but Nisa saw the gleam of respect in his eyes.

"Not many," he said at last. "Not many at all."

After a quick tour of the house, Nisa grabbed her keys and led Ty back outside. She locked the door and they climbed into her truck.

"Where are we going?" he asked.

"You'll see." She turned the key in the ignition, shifting the manual transmission into reverse as she backed out of the driveway.

"You're not gonna give me any clues?"

Nisa giggled. "What? You don't trust me?"

Ty grabbed the 'oh crap!' handle attached to the ceiling above the door and braced himself against the dash with the other. The muscles in his brawny forearms flexed with each movement. "There. I do now."

She pretended to be hurt as she headed back into the city. "And here I thought I was a good driver," she quipped. "Cole taught me himself."

Grinning, he released the handle. "Well, since it was Cole…"

"You jerk." She risked a sidelong glance at him as she turned left at the light.

He laughed. "I've been called worse, darlin'."

"I'm sure." She smirked. "Probably by Cole."

"You're probably right."

Nisa was silent as she maneuvered her little pickup through traffic, shifting lanes as she drove through the marsh.

"La Crosse is nice," he said.

"I really like it here." Nisa waited for the traffic to clear as she idled in the left-turn lane onto Main Street. She gunned the motor and sailed through the intersection as the light turned yellow. "We might make it." She turned onto the winding lane that led to the top of the lookout point.

"Make it where?"

"You'll see." She navigated Bliss Road as it wound up the bluff. The smells of beer and fried foods of the Alpine Inn greeted her as she made the last hard-right turn leading to the park.

"Oh wow," Ty breathed. "This reminds me of the Blue Ridge Parkway."

Forest and thicket lined both sides of the narrow lane as she guided her truck toward their ultimate destination. "I bet."

The lane finally widened into a parking lot, and Nisa found an open spot close to the shelter. "We're here."

Nisa turned off the motor and hopped out of the truck, following the path around the shelter leading to the city's highest point. The crunch of gravel beneath footsteps indicated that Ty was right behind her as she went to an open spot along the fence. She braced her arms on the rail and gazed out to the west over the city as the sun sank toward the horizon. "Welcome to Granddad Bluff," she said as Ty mimicked her pose.

"Stunning."

His breath tickled her ear and she turned, her lips a hair's breadth from his. She could taste his breath on hers. Sometime between the restaurant and now he'd popped a breath mint. His blue eyes turned intense again.

"What?" she asked. "Me or the sunset?"

Ty gave her another sexy smile. "Yes."

Nisa wanted very much to kiss him again, but not with so many people around. Instead, she pointed across the river. "See those bluffs over there? That's Minnesota." She turned to the south, where twilight had already darkened the sky. "And those headlands in the distance? That's Iowa."

"Which ones?"

Ty's voice was husky as she turned back to him. She hadn't expected him to be that close, and her body rocked into his. He immediately wrapped her in his arms,

"Easy, darlin'," he whispered, brushing her lips with his.

"Excuse me."

The voice of a child broke the spell Ty had woven around her.

"Mr. Patterson? Could I have your autograph, please?"

"Sure," Ty said, letting Nisa go.

Nisa noted the change that came over him. He seemed more aloof, and somehow his smile didn't quite reach his eyes as he signed a picture for the little boy, and posed for a few more. She made sure to stay well in the background like she'd wanted to during the race. He talked about the upcoming race with the kid's dad and a couple other guys milling about, until Ty finally extricated himself. He thanked them again for their support, and made a point to shake the little boy's hand one more time before returning to her side.

"I'm sorry," Nisa whispered. "I didn't realize there would be so many people up here."

"It's okay." Ty shrugged. "I'm used to it."

Having been with Cole a number of times when he'd been mobbed by fans, Nisa knew that the drivers who had established themselves in NASCAR's highest ranks were always sought out by autograph-seekers and fame-hunters, even if the limelight shone no farther than their circle of friends. "Ready to go?" she asked.

He nodded. "Thank you for bringing me up here."

"You're welcome."

As they walked back to the parking lot, he took her hand in his. "Come with me to Michigan."

"I – I can't," she whispered, unlocking the truck as a strange emotion pierced her heart.

"Can't?" he asked, caging her against the door with his body. "Or won't?"

"I'm not ready." She shook her head. "It's all going too fast."

"What is?"

"This. Us."

"Are you still hung up on my job?"

She flinched.

"Because that's all it is. A job that I do. One I happen to love."

Nisa shook her head. She knew better. "Ty, you can't fool me. Racing isn't just a job. It's a way of life. It consumes you. It gets into your soul. Your blood. Until all you can think about is the next race. The next win. The fast pace doesn't stop after the last flag drops at Homestead." She took a breath. "I know how hard the teams work all year round. My dad had one of the best pair of hands in the biz, whether he was behind the wheel or under the hood.”

Darkness had fallen over the bluff and they were the only ones left in the parking lot.

“Tell me, Nisa.” He pulled out the elastic band and threaded his fingers through her hair. “What are you so afraid of?”

Chapter 12

Ty's question haunted Nisa for the rest of the week as she finalized her designs for the Love's Kiss collection. It wasn't even Father's Day, and she was already planning for Valentine's Day. Her shoulders slumped in sadness at the reminder of her dad, and she nearly burst into tears. She called her boss, requesting the day off. Putting away her sketch pad, she grabbed her purse and headed for her truck.

Nisa slotted the key into the ignition and cranked the motor. She shifted into reverse and was about to back out of the parking stall, when the dam burst from the song pouring through the speakers.

She shifted the transmission back into neutral and let the pickup idle as she leaned her head against the steering wheel and cried. "Wind Beneath My Wings" had always been Angela's favorite song, but Daddy had played it so much after she'd died that Nisa associated the haunting melody with both of them. And the gaping hole in her life by their deaths, which were thirteen months apart.

There were times when Nisa thought she'd moved on and, if only partially, filled that emotional void. Others, like now, she'd be blindsided by reminders and the debilitating pain would sear her again, fresh and raw.

When the sobs subsided, her whole body ached and her throat burned. Nisa swallowed, wincing, feeling like she'd gargled with glass shards. She jumped from the sharp rap against her window, her foot nearly slipping off the brake.

A man about Cole's age motioned for her to open her window. His salt-and-pepper hair was thick, the strands waving in the slight breeze. Nisa wiped her eyes and cracked open the window to the edge of the vent visor.

"Are you okay, miss?" he asked, concern clouding his warm brown eyes.

"I am now," she replied, wiping her sleeve across her cheek. "Thank you."

The man nodded and walked away.

Nice guy. Nisa removed the last traces of her tears and shifted the transmission into reverse, heading home. Pulling into her driveway twenty minutes later, she parked the truck and entered the small three-bedroom house. She called her friend as she rummaged through the fridge for a pre-dinner snack.

"Hey, Emmie." Not finding anything really appealing, she grabbed a cup of peach Greek yogurt from the bottom drawer. "What are you doing for dinner tonight?" The connection crackled, and she only caught a couple words. "What?"

"I said, I'm not doing anything," Emmie repeated. "What's up?"

"I – want to go somewhere for dinner?" Nisa closed the door and snatched a spoon from the strainer on the counter, still full from the last time she did dishes.

"Sure," Emmie said. "Where do you want to go?"

Nisa shrugged, tearing the foil lid off her yogurt and stirred it with her spoon. "I dunno. I hadn't gotten that far."

Emmie chuckled. "Pick me up, and we'll go from there."

"Sounds good. See you in a bit."

Nisa hung up and changed out of her work clothes, pulling on some yoga pants and the t-shirt she'd picked up in Charlotte, then shoved her feet into sneakers, all between bites of the thick, creamy yogurt. Fifteen minutes later she pulled up in front of Emmie's apartment building and rang the doorbell.

"Hey, hon." Emmie stepped to the side and Nisa entered the apartment.

"Hey. You ready?"

"Yeah. Let me grab my purse." Emmie disappeared down the short hallway to her bedroom.

"Where are you going?" Emmie's son, Kevin, asked.

Nisa bristled at the accusing tone in his voice. "I don't know yet," she said, keeping her tone light. "We haven't decided."

"Make her call me when she gets there." He turned and stomped back into his own bedroom.

Emmie returned moments later and they headed for the truck.

"Why do you let your son bully you like that?" Nisa asked, concerned for her friend. Emmie's family didn't deserve her.

"Because … I don't know." Emmie shrugged. "Because he learned it from his father."

"Oh, honey." She vowed to give Emmie a hug. "You can stay with me any time you want to get away from them."

"It's not that easy," Emmie said despairingly. "Let's just drop it."

Emmie was close to tears, so Nisa agreed. She silently promised herself to keep her friend out as long as she could, given that they both had to work in the morning. "Let's go see a movie," she said instead. "My treat."

"What do you want to see?"

"Well." Nisa grinned. "There's always the new Channing Tatum flick."

Emmie grinned, her personal problems temporarily forgotten. "Oh, hell yeah!"

Nisa suggested sushi for dinner knowing Emmie couldn't bring herself to try it even though she and Shayla both loved it.

"No way!" Emmie exclaimed. "Anything but that!"

Nisa laughed. "How do gyros sound instead?"

"Better."

Nisa headed for Gracie's over by UW-La Crosse. After dinner they made for the only movie theater left in town.

"Have you thought any more about Ty?" Emmie asked.

"Every day," Nisa said truthfully. He'd addressed every one of her concerns without making light of her fears. The more time she spent in his company the more layers she'd peeled away. She'd been with the racecar driver, the persona he'd displayed for the media and his fans but she'd also been with the man behind the façade. The more time she'd spent with him, the deeper in love she fell.

"Have you decided what you're going to do?"

Nisa shook her head as she turned into the parking lot and found an empty space. "Not yet."

"What are you waiting for?" Emmie asked. "A prime specimen like that won't be single much longer. The more you wait the better chance you have of losing him."

Nisa killed the motor of her pickup. "It's not that easy." She repeated Emmie's words from earlier, climbing out of the truck. "I'm still having a hard time dealing with the fact that he's not only a stock car driver, but he's Cole's biggest rival."

"The heart wants what the heart wants." Emmie followed as Nisa headed for the entrance. "Do you love him?"

A sharp pain pierced Nisa's heart. "I think I might." She'd only known Ty for a few weeks, but she couldn't believe how strong her emotions were for him in such a short time.

"Then you'll have to find a way to get past your fears so you can be with him."

"Thank you, Captain Obvious." Nisa winced at her petulant tone. "I'm sorry. I know what I need to do, but I'm not sure how to go about getting there."

"Well, spending time with him would be a good start."

Nisa paid for the tickets and they waited in line at the concession stand. "I did that in Charlotte, and he came to La Crosse on Tuesday."

"He was in town and you didn't say anything?" Emmie squealed as they accepted their popcorn and sodas.

Nisa looked sheepish. "He stopped to see me at work." She took a sip of her drink. "I overheard him and Viktor talking about jewelry. They went into a private consultation room and I went to lunch."

Emmie practically jumped up and down. "Did he –"

"No, he didn't." Nisa sat down in a middle chair about two-thirds of the way up the inclined seating. "Honestly, I don't think he knew I was there when he approached my boss."

"Wait. I don't understand," Emmie said in a low voice. "He talked to your boss about a piece of jewelry, but he didn't ask you to marry him? And he didn't even present you with anything?"

Nisa shook her head. "That about sums it up."

"That's crazy!" Emmie nearly leapt out of her seat." Why would he do that?"

"Shh!" The gal in front of them turned and put her finger over her lips. "Quiet!"

"Sheesh!" Emmie said in a stage whisper. "The movie hasn't even started yet."

Nisa giggled. The woman gave them another death glare.

"So what's your next move?" Emmie asked in a quieter voice.

Nisa popped a couple buttery kernels into her mouth and wiped her oily fingertips on a napkin. "I don't know."

"Seems to me like you should go to the race."

"Mmm." Nisa made a noncommittal response, even as the wheels in her brain began churning. Making a note to contact Cole's PR rep, she leaned back in her seat and grew silent as the opening credits began rolling.

****

"You nearly hit the wall on that last turn," Pete said as Ty grabbed a bottle of water from the mini fridge in the galley.

As much respect Ty had for his crew chief, he couldn't help rolling his eyes. And received a punch on the arm for his efforts. "It was all I could do to keep her off the wall." He rubbed the spot where Pete hit him, despite the light tap. "She was way too loose in three and four." Wrenching the cap off the bottle, he took a deep swallow.

"We'll work on adjustments for next practice." Pete scribbled something on his ever-present clipboard, a throwback from before crew chiefs started using laptops. "How's it goin' with Forester's sister?"

"She's still holdin' back." Ty finished his water and tossed the bottle into the recycling bin.

"Her dad?" Pete looked up from his notes.

"I think so." He hesitated. "Partly."

"Have you talked to Cole?"

"I have, but only about her favorite foods." Ty shook his head. "I didn't have the time to ask him about courtin' her."

Pete leveled his gaze at Ty. "Do you plan on it?"

"I don't know." Ty shrugged under his crew chief's scrutiny. "I probably should. Maybe he can help."

"Maybe, if he doesn't have a problem with you sniffin' 'round his sister." Pete turned back to his notes, his pen scribbling furiously. "See you out there."

Ty nodded. He headed to the conference room at the front of the hauler and sprawled out on the couch, his head on the armrest. Closing his eyes, he pictured the track in his mind, trying to imagine his preferred line around the slick surface. Instead, clear emerald-green eyes and auburn hair blurred his vision. He growled in frustration and shoved off the sofa, dragging his hands through his hair. He paced a couple laps around the lounge like a caged tiger, then went back to the garage. What he really wanted to do was run a few laps around the two-mile track on foot to burn off the energy pumping through him.

A hand clapped on his shoulder. He jumped, turning to see who it was. The fight left him. "Hey, Cole."

"Ty." Cole's voice was terse. "Have you heard from my sister?"

His guard came back up at the question. "I saw her on Tuesday, but I haven't talked to her since." He considered his crew chief's words from earlier. "Maybe you can help. She seems hesitant about a relationship with me." He chose his words carefully, letting Cole know that he wanted something more than a fling with Nisa. "I'm trying to make her see how good we are together, but she seems scared."

Cole was silent for a moment, appearing to consider his words as they walked down Hauler Row. "I don't think it's you," he said at last, "though I wouldn't blame her if it was."

Ty ignored the dig. "Is it our job?"

"More than likely, considering our family history. My sister's her own woman." Cole waved to Ty's teammate, Dominic Sands, as they passed his hauler.

"Did I miss something?" Dom interrupted their conversation. "I don't need to play referee, do I?"

Cole laughed. "Nah, man. We're cool."

"Never thought I'd see the day." Dom scrubbed his hand over his chin. "You two getting along."

"Don't get used to it." Ty smirked.

"I bet." Dom tipped the bill of his cap at them. "See you on the track."

Ty waved to his teammate as they resumed walking.

"Talk to Nisa. If this is what she wants, I support both of you." Cole resumed their conversation. "But you better treat her right."

That went without saying.

Ty relaxed. As much as he could in work mode, anyway. As hard as Cole raced, he always did it clean. Ty hated to admit it, but a grudging respect for his fiercest rival began blooming in his chest. The man was loyal. To his team, and to his family. Ty winced.

They went their separate ways at the entrance to the garage. As Ty entered his stall, the full brunt of Nisa's predicament hit him hard in the gut. Cole was all the family she had left.

But you could offer her yours. His grandmother would love nothing more than to see him settle down with a good woman. And Nisa certainly qualified as one.

The thought wove through his brain and his heart, hardening his resolve as he approached his team.

****

Nisa crossed the parking lot after work and unlocked the door to her truck. She'd opened the door and was about to get in when a voice from behind stopped her.

"Nice truck."

She turned, and greeted her former classmate Quinn Jackson. "Thanks, Quinn."

"Hey, Marie." He walked around her truck, open admiration in his gaze. "Five-speed manual. I'm impressed."

Nisa smirked. She wasn't fooled. While every other truck had horses beneath the hood, her customized Ranger had hamsters. "You should look past the paint job." She shrugged. "Besides, ya can't call it a real truck unless it has a stick."

"True," Quinn agreed. "I'm surprised you got one, that's all."

"What?" She cocked a brow. "A truck? Or the manual transmission?"

"Both, actually." He grinned, his teeth blinding against his orange hair and freckles.

"Please." Nisa rolled her eyes. "I've been driving a manual for fifteen years."

His eyes lit up. "You learned on a stick?"

Nisa gave him a small smile. "Should've seen my first one."

He ran a finger over the custom pinstripe along the side of the bed. She shivered, remembering the day she'd gotten her baby back from the paint shop. She'd had the body painted a metallic purple, then had a combination of her dad's and brother's racing colors in a swirl along either side of the bed. The swirls converged into a checkered flag along the top of the tailgate above the handle, blending into a pair of angel's wings that spread across the entire tailgate.

"What was your first car?"

Nisa blinked, bringing herself out of the memory. She gave him a smile of genuine amusement. "It was better than yours," she couldn't help boasting. In high school Quinn had one of the best cars in the lot, a brand-new Jeep Liberty tricked out with the ultimate off-road package.

"I highly doubt that." Obviously he was sharing her memory. "What was it?"

"A brand-new Two-Thousand-Six Chevy Monte Carlo SS. Souped up, stripped down. No A/C, no radio." Except for the one that let her talk with Cole and Will. "Three-fifty big block motor bored out to a three-fifty-eight, seven hundred and fifty horsepower." Nisa watched Quinn's eyes glaze over. "Top speed about two-twenty unrestricted, one eighty-five restricted. No windows or doors."

Disbelief replaced the gearhead lust. "Yeah, right. That's not street-legal. And why would you restrict the motor, anyway?"

"Safety." Nisa grinned.

"How?"

"Choke the carb."

"Huh?"

Nisa laughed at his blank expression. For a race fan, he wasn't catching on very fast. "Put a restrictor plate between the carburetor and the intake manifold. Cuts air flow to the motor, decreasing horsepower."

"Wait." Realization slowly dawned. "You only do that with racecars."

"Very good. And only at Talladega and Daytona."

Quinn's eyes bugged. "Your first ride was a stock car?"

She nodded, studying her classmate's face. The admiration was back, mixed with respect, yet also some of his doubt remained.

"Did you go to one of those driving experience things?" he asked.

"No. It was my brother's car." Nisa shook her head. "I got to drive the real thing. In real racing conditions." She had been suppressing her past for so long that it suddenly became difficult to share those details with a man who had claimed she wasn't good enough to date his friend. "At Dover."

"No way!" Quinn exclaimed. "Your brother drives NASCAR? Who is he?"

She kept her expression carefully blank, knowing it would probably make him change the way he felt about her. "Cole Forester."

"Wow! And your dad was Gary." His expression altered into a swaggering-peacock grin, and his stance shifted to imply overinflated importance.

She nodded again. Yep. He was changing his opinion of her. "It gave me great pleasure to hear you talk racing with your friends," she continued, keeping her tone light. "You continually touted my dad as one of your favorites, not even realizing his daughter was right under your nose." She smiled sadly. "Though you gave me a couple sideways glances when I first arrived in Onalaska."

"And you introduced yourself as Marie instead."

"My full name is Anissa Marie Forester."

Quinn compressed his lips. "Incognito?"

"Not really." She shrugged again. "More like a new place, a fresh start. A chance to get away from the spotlight."

Quinn grimaced, remorse coloring his expression. And a hint of chagrin. "I'm so sorry, Marie. I never realized."

"It's okay, Quinn. I'm over it." She turned to leave.

"Wait." He put his hand on her arm. "Wanna get a cup of coffee or something?"

I was right. Telling him the truth about her past had changed how he felt about her. In some ways it was a positive change, but it also saddened her at the same time, making her question his motives for asking. "Why would you want to have coffee with a –" *what had he called me in high school?* "–scheming little parasite?"

Quinn had the grace to blush. "Give me a chance to apologize. Though honestly, I didn't really think that of you. Neither did Ryan. I think some of the other guys still do.”

Standing tall, she straightened her shoulders. “It doesn’t matter anymore. I’m over it.”

“Then have coffee, or whatever, with me.”

“Fine.” Nisa locked her truck and they walked to the coffee shop at the corner of Fourth and Pearl. She ordered her usual white mocha and pumpkin bread, then waited at the end of the counter while Quinn made his selection. A few minutes later the barista handed them their steaming mugs and they found an empty table on the outdoor patio.

“So … Anissa.” He stumbled a moment over her Christian name. “That’s gonna take some getting used to.”

Nisa allowed herself a small half-smile. “I’ll bet.”

“What was it like?” he asked, sipping from his mug.

“What?” she knitted her brow.

“Never mind.” He shook his head, his mop of carrot-colored curls fluttering in the slight breeze. “I was trying to ask about your dad. But you don’t have to answer if you don’t want to.”

“It’s okay.” Nisa sipped her mocha. “Honestly, I’d like to talk about him.” Even if it was with one of the people who’d made high school a living hell for her. After her weekend she found that she could talk about her dad without the pain and anguish of her childhood. "He was a great man. Even twenty years ago he knew how to cater to his fans and sponsors. He was the best of both worlds."

"What was that?"

"He's a carry-over from the roots of NASCAR, but he was also a visionary. I don't think even he realized how popular the sport would become or the huge amounts of money that would be poured into it, but he had an idea." Nisa nibbled a bite of her pumpkin bread. "He saw how extensive the media coverage had become, between print, radio and television, even in the eighties. Suddenly backyard garage mechanics became household names overnight. Winners were remembered across the country, not only in their hometown or among fans at the track." She sipped her coffee. "And he was one of the first drivers to embrace the new era. He taught Cole how to embrace it, too." She flashed a sad smile. "That same media can become fickle in a heartbeat. The moment my dad hit the wall, everything changed. On the track, in the infield. The whole world of NASCAR."

"And for you personally." Understanding darkened Quinn's eyes to the color of cobalt.

She nodded. "Irrevocably." And that, she realized, was the biggest reason why she was so scared to become involved with Tyson Patterson.

"So, what are you going to do now?" Quinn asked, interrupting her thoughts.

"I don't know. I guess keep going the way I have been." *With your life, but what about Ty?* The voice in the back of her mind refused to be silenced. "Though maybe I'll make a few changes." Nisa drained her mug.

Quinn emptied his too. "Will you go back to NASCAR?"

"In a way I already have." Nisa stared at a speck of silver on the wrought-iron table. "I went back to Charlotte for Memorial Day. The press took notice and asked me for interviews, which I declined." But they would probably start asking questions again if she and Ty made their relationship public.

"I saw the tribute to your dad," Quinn said softly. "I wondered why you stood next to Cole."

"And now you know."

Quinn nodded. "He was a good man."

"Yes, he was." Nisa fell silent for a few moments. "I'm scared to go back," she said at last.

"Why?"

"I guess I've been my own identity for so long that if I go back I'll no longer be Nisa Forester. I'll be Gary's daughter and Cole's sister again."

"But you never stopped being a daughter and sister," Quinn pointed out. "You never stopped being Anissa Forester, even if you spent the last twenty years going by Marie."

Nisa cocked her head to the side. He had her attention.

"They'll always be a part of you," he explained. "Of who you are. You can't run from that, no matter how much you try."

She sighed. He had a point. Damn it! "Then I guess it's time to stop trying to." In more ways than one. She ran the upcoming race schedule in her mind. Cole and Ty had an off-week after the next three races. She hoped Ty didn't have any plans, because she was quickly formulating her return to Charlotte. "Thank you, Quinn." She reached out and put her hand over his, surprising both of them with the contact. "You've helped me more than you could ever realize."

They talked about high school for a bit longer. His apology for his behavior back then caught her off-guard, but she accepted it with a wave of her hand. She'd told him the truth when she'd said she was over it. She hadn't given it – them – much thought since graduation.

Nisa headed back to her truck. She had some calls to make when she got home.

****

"The balance feels off," Ty said, climbing from his car after the practice run at Michigan.

Pete scribbled notes on the pages attached to his clipboard. "Where?"

"Left side," Ty answered. "She feels like she's lifting going into the corners."

"We'll get it fixed." Pete went off to talk with one of the engineers.

Ty returned to the hauler and grabbed his third bottle of water for the day, fighting off the humid early-summer heat as he retreated to the air conditioning of the War Room. It was his favorite places besides behind the wheel. A techie's paradise, a huge HD plasma television spanned almost the full length of one wall, while banks of computers lined up on a table beneath the television. On a shelf beneath the table sat two top-level video gaming systems with controllers, and several multi-player games for both systems lined up on the shelf next to them. There were several ports around the entire room that would recharge any electronic device imaginable. And they could even hook up any computer to the television.

An oak conference table was bolted to the floor in the center, and leather couches lined the walls on either side and the back wall facing the television. Ty flopped onto the long sofa and leaned against the armrest, stretching his legs out in front of him, opening the bottle and taking a long drink of the cold water. He recapped the bottle and closed his eyes, absorbing the silence around him as his racing heart returned to normal.

Then auburn hair and green eyes once again flashed behind his closed eyelids. His chat with Cole hadn't gone as expected. Maybe that's a good thing. He shoved his hands through his hair in frustration, then launched himself off the sofa, suddenly too restless to stand still.

He finished off his water and tossed the bottle into the nearly-full recycling bin, anxious to get back out with his crew. Even though they preferred that he didn't help with the adjustments. He trusted them implicitly to get the corrections made and ready for Sunday's race.

As luck would have it, Ty's garage stall was next to Cole's, being that they were three and four in the current points standings. But Ty was only seven points behind, and planned to take third before they went to the road course in

California's Wine Country. He sent a polite nod toward his rival. Cole returned the greeting, his expression grim. Anxiety churned in Ty's gut as he wondered if that look was about him dating Nisa. He pushed it aside and focused on the car.

Ty climbed out of the car after the final practice round ended, but there was still plenty of work to do before tomorrow's race. He still felt that the weight balance was off, but the handling was getting better. He could fly into the turns without feeling like he was going to sail into the outer catch fence.

"What do you want for dinner?" Pete asked, packing away the laptops and locking down the garage for the night.

Ty grinned. "How about that place in Jackson? I'm sure they still have tripe on the menu."

Pete suddenly looked a little green around the gills. "No freaking way."

Ty put his crew chief in a headlock as they walked toward the hauler. "I'm kidding. How does Italian sound?"

"Better."

Before they could get to the hauler, they were mobbed by fans and reporters. Ty scrawled his name across a few items that were thrust his way, keeping his momentum going forward as he answered the reporters' questions. He and Pete made it to the back door of the hauler and escaped into the sanctuary, exchanging wry smiles.

Dinner that night was boisterous, the team in high spirits. Ty was quiet, letting Pete carry the conversation. Ty could only think about Nisa, and how much he wanted her with him. She kept putting him off about their next time together, and frustration ate him alive. His hand went to the cell phone clipped to his belt. Later, he promised himself.

"…so this guy comes over and throws a big, black hairy spider in Dom's car while he's strapped in," Pete said chuckling. "And of course Dom wears that yellow and white suit."

Ty chuckled at the memory. "The next thing I know, Dom's got his safety gear unhooked and he's flying out of the car like his ass is on fire, screaming 'Get it off!' at the top of his lungs."

His crew laughed. He looked around the table at the men he considered his family, but instead of feeling content or a sense of accomplishment at his career achievements, he only felt a restlessness he couldn't dispel. He did his best to push it aside as they all paid for their meals and headed for the door. A hand on his arm stopped Ty as he reached the entrance. He turned.

"Excuse me," said the young woman. "Are you Ty Patterson?"

He gave her his camera-ready smile and nodded. "What can I do for you?"

Color infused her face. She was petite, only coming to his chest. It took him a moment to realize she held something out for him. He took the photo from her and scribbled his name across the page, exchanging inane platitudes and thanking her before heading back to the van where his team waited.

His front tire carrier put him in a headlock and knuckled the top of his head. "You dog!"

Ty fake-punched his crew member in the gut and slid easily from his grasp, chuckling at the good-natured ribbing. "Careful, man," he warned. "You might end up with a nasty surprise when you least expect it."

The guys were still jovial on the drive back, but Ty couldn't keep from falling back into his reflective mood, his thoughts returning to Nisa.

"Dude!" Pete grabbed Ty's arm. "Call her already."

Ty groaned and buried his head in his arm as he endured another round of ribbing. "Not in front of you clowns."

That earned him more razzing. He laughed, ducking as napkin balls flew at his head.

"Since when is the infallible Tyson Patterson hung up over a woman?"

The taunt came from somewhere in the back, but Ty didn't turn and look at the heckler. He looked out the window instead, saying nothing.

"Chill, guys," Pete said in his no-nonsense voice. "She is not part of shop talk. She deserves respect, especially since Ty's interested in dating her."

Maybe more. The thought hit Ty in the left temple, lodged in his brain and took root.

The crew protested, but Pete put them back in their place. Ty grinned, remembering the pact they'd made about respecting the wives and girlfriends of the other guys on the team.

"Hey!" Pete shouted over the ruckus. "You wouldn't want us to talk about your women like that, would you?"

Ty almost snickered at how quiet the interior of the van got.

"Do we know her?" the front tire changer asked.

"You might know of her." Ty glanced back from the front passenger seat. "She's Cole Forester's sister."

"Oh, man." The whispered words echoed in the heavy silence.

"Exactly," Ty pounced. "Now you know what I'm up against."

Ty's crew issued a chorus of apology as Pete drove through the tunnel of the infield. As soon as they pulled into the Drivers and Owners lot, the change from goof-off to work mode was like the flip of a switch.

If Ty wasn't so tied up in knots over Nisa, he might've laughed. He went to his motor coach and punched in the security code on the keypad. After locking up for the night, he went to the spacious bedroom at the back of his home away from home and stripped down, slipping beneath the blankets.

But his thoughts were so jumbled he couldn't fall asleep.

Chapter 13

Ten weeks later anxiety and excitement churned in the pit of Nisa's stomach as Cole's team jet touched down at the Charlotte-Douglas International Airport.

Cole's last call four days ago had been cryptic, and she hadn't been able to reach him since. Bittersweet memories assailed her senses as she crossed the tarmac to the waiting limo.

The driver stowed her overnight case and opened the door for her. The air-conditioned comfort of the luxury car's interior was refreshing after the sultry late-August heat. Nisa leaned back into the soft leather and closed her eyes, trying unsuccessfully to steady her nerves. The engine started and the tires hummed softly over the pavement. The soft swish of rubber over asphalt was a soothing balm to her frayed nerves.

Images flitted behind her closed eyelids as the limo driver headed for their destination. Her father hoisting her onto his shoulders in Victory Lane. Angela's funeral, then Dad's a year later. Ty's strong arms wrapped around her as they danced. His mouth moving over hers in a kiss that stole her breath. The sunset they shared in La Crosse.

Ty said her name over and over, his hands caressing her face, neck, back and shoulders. The silky strands of his hair flowed like water through her fingers.

"Nisa," Ty whispered in her ear. "Come back to me, honey."

I love you, Ty,

"I love you too, sweetheart." He jostled her again. "Come on. Wake up."

Nisa slowly fluttered her eyes open, confusion fogging her mind as she found herself back in the limo. The images had seemed so real. "Ty?" she asked drowsily. *Oh, God. Did I say that out loud?* Her mouth felt like it was packed with cotton. "Where am I?" She slowly sat up and looked around. "Where's Cole?"

"We're at my place," he said. "We'll meet with Cole later."

"Why?" The word rattled around in her sleep-addled brain.

Ty kissed her forehead. "We can talk about it when you're fully awake." He slid off the sofa and headed for the hallway.

Nisa slid the elastic from her hair and combed her fingers through the curling tresses before rubbing the sleep from her eyes.

Ty returned a minute later and handed her a glass. "This should help wake you up."

She took the glass and sniffed. "What is it?"

His eyes crinkled at the corners. "Water."

Embarrassed, heat flooded her face. "Oh. Sorry."

"No worries."

She took a long drink as Ty sat next to her on the sofa. The cool water dispelled most of her tiredness, and his nearness took care of the rest. Every nerve ending sizzled to life as he brushed a lock of hair behind her ear.

"I'm glad you're here," he whispered. "I've missed you."

He pulled back as she closed in for a kiss. She knitted her brow, confusion flitting through her. "Is something wrong?"

He shook his head "No, but this is too important to not do the right way."

"Do what?" She pushed off the sofa. "Ty, what's going on?"

"Everything's fine, sweetheart." He stood as well. "But trust me, okay? I don't want to ruin the surprise because I know it's something you'll love."

Nisa considered her options, then slowly nodded. "Fine." She sighed. "Where's Cole? I thought I was meeting him at his house?"

"The limo driver had instructions to bring you here." Ty gently rubbed her arms.

"Wait." Nisa stepped back, crossing her arms over her chest. "So, I was brought here under false pretenses?"

"What? No!" He sounded outraged. "Nisa, Cole asked you to come back for me. I wanted to surprise you, Take you out on a date."

"Then why didn't you ask?" Fury pumped through her, hot and strong. "Why the subterfuge?"

"This isn't going as I'd hoped." Ty shoved his hands through his hair. "Can we start over?" he begged. "Please?"

"What's going on, Ty?" she asked. "What's your plan?"

Ty flinched at her harsh tone. "I want to take you shopping, then out to dinner where we'll meet up with Cole."

"Why shopping?" She didn't let up.

"I had hoped tonight would be as much a special occasion for you as it is for me." He pulled her into his arms. "Please, Nisa. Let's stick to the plan, okay? I love you so much, and I want this for you so badly."

Her eyes bugged as a tidal wave of hope drowned out the fury. "You love me?"

"Yes, I do." His expression softened. "I was going to tell you for the first time over dinner."

"A special occasion," she confirmed.

Ty grinned. "Yeah. I think that telling a woman I love her for the first time happens to be pretty special."

"I think so, too." She felt foolish. "Okay, Ty. Let's stick to the plan and go to dinner."

"Wait." Ty caressed her arms again.

Her heart sank a little. She held her breath, saying nothing.

"You haven't told me you love me back." He frowned. "Unless I'm wrong and you don't love me."

"But I do!" Nisa flung her arms around his neck. "I love you so much it hurts!"

"I can't tell you how happy I am to hear you say that."

He kissed her neck, hugging her close. Threading his fingers through her hair, Ty gently cupped the back of her head and lifted her face to his. Their gazes locked the moment before he claimed her lips in a kiss that turned her blood to molten lava in her veins. They were both breathing hard when he broke away, and her heart pounded in her chest.

"Let's go to dinner," he said.

She walked her fingers over the contours of his rock-hard chest. "Or we can stay in and celebrate." His breath hitched and she giggled.

"No." Ty captured her hand with his. "Shopping, then dinner."

She gave him her best fake pout. "The plan."

"You're so cute when you're in a snit." He kissed the tip of her nose. "Yes, we need to stick to the plan."

Nisa tried to get mad at him for real, but knowing he loved her drowned out every other emotion. Ty ushered her out to his car. He took her to an upscale boutique in Mooresville and told her to pick out whatever she wanted.

Nisa looked around, overwhelmed. Every color and women's fashion designer available hung on the racks. Ty explained to the employees that his girlfriend needed a new dress for the evening. As soon as he was recognized, every salesgirl in the store flocked to them, each insisting they had the perfect dress. Nisa flashed a wry smirk at Ty, highly doubtful of the associates' selections. She shook her head. As she suspected, they didn't know her well enough to choose her clothing. Retail therapy had never interested her, and anxiety stole over her body. She had to get away from the attention. The salesgirls continued showing their gown ideas, until a plump brunette with warm gray eyes approached Nisa empty-handed.

"I'm Sharita, the store manager. I understand you're looking for a dress," she said as another eager salesgirl approached with a dress swirled with hideous shades of orange, tan and brown. The woman shooed the girl away with a flick of her wrist. "You don't want that one."

Nisa nodded. "Thank you."

"Do you have something in mind?" Sharita asked.

"Not really." Nisa hesitated. "The date was sort of … um… sprung on me literally at the last minute."

"What type of restaurant?" The woman didn't back down.

Nisa hesitated, and Ty stepped in. "It's relatively upscale, but still casual. A cocktail dress will be fine."

"Come with me, dear." Sharita gently but firmly took Nisa's arm. "Let's find something more suitable."

"Thank you." Nisa could only hope that this woman had better taste than the younger staff.

After Sharita asked a few questions about Nisa's size and color preference, they stopped at a large circular rack. It was a special occasion, so Nisa tried hard to stay away from black as she rifled through the rail. A dress in vermilion silk caught her eye and she pulled the hanger off the bar. The cut was simple, the bodice in a wraparound style with a deep V-neck and a gently flared skirt that would swirl around Ty's legs if he were to spin her around on the dance floor. She imagined the three-quarter-length sleeves caressing her flesh like a lover's touch, the wine color bringing out the red highlights in her auburn hair.

"Great choice."

Nisa jumped. She'd almost forgotten the other woman was still there.

"Perfect," Ty agreed. "I can't wait to see you wearing it."

"Would you like to try it on?" Sharita asked.

Nisa nodded, and the other woman led her to the changing rooms at the back of the boutique. Closeted in her cubicle, an inexplicable shyness overcame her. Nisa suddenly didn't want Ty to see her until she dressed for their date, but she still wanted a second opinion.

"Sharita?" she called.

"What can I help you with?" the manager asked.

"Could you tell Ty to wait in front, please?" Nisa asked. "I don't want him to see it yet."

"Of course."

"Why not?" Ty asked.

Was that worry in his voice? Nisa smiled, her mind whirling for the perfect answer. "Consider it part of the plan," she said, recalling his words from earlier.

He chuckled, and she relaxed. "As you wish."

Nisa quickly stripped down to her underwear, a utilitarian white lace bra and matching granny panties, and cringed at her reflection. *I'm glad I have sexy underwear in my bag.* She slipped the dress over her head and settled it over her curves, adjusting as needed for the proper fit. The fabric skimmed rather than clung, whispering over her flesh.

She turned, looking from as many angles as she could within the limited confines of the dressing room. Her panty line stood out like a sore thumb and she made a face.

"Is everything all right?"

Sharita's voice broke through Nisa's thoughts. "Yeah."

With one last fortifying breath, she stepped out of the dressing room.

Sharita's whistle carried throughout the store. "Honey, you're gonna knock his socks off."

"Nisa?" Ty's voice came from the racks to her left. "Are you okay?"

"I'm fine," she called out. "Please don't come closer."

"Trust me, dollface." Sharita raised her voice to address Ty. "When you see her, your mind will be blown." She turned back to Nisa. "Among other things."

Nisa giggled at the endearment, and her comment.

"Let's complete your outfit, dear." Sharita pushed Nisa back into the dressing room. "Get changed."

"Yes, ma'am!" Nisa smarted off to the manager as she disappeared behind the curtain.

"You're lucky I don't have a towel," Sharita called out. "Ty'd find a burn mark on your behind for a week!"

Nisa joked back as she stripped carefully from the dress. "Then I'm glad you don't!" She put her own clothes back on and slipped into her shoes. She stepped out of the cubicle, the dress draped over her arm.

"I don't have any shoes to go with this dress," Sharita said, "but it deserves silver or black. There's a shoe store two doors down."

Ty and Nisa went to the register with Sharita, and the older woman swiped Ty's credit card.

"You take her to that store, ya hear?" She passed the credit card back to Ty. "Treat this gal right."

Nisa fidgeted under Ty's scrutiny as he tucked the card into his wallet. She really didn't want him spending his money on her.

"That's my plan." Ty laid his hand on her back. "Thank you for everything, Sharita."

"Anytime, dollface."

Ty laughed as he ushered Nisa to the door, the heat from his touch searing her flesh through her thin blouse.

"You don't have to take me to that store," she said once they were outside. "I brought a pair of shoes."

"No way, babe." He grinned. "You're gonna knock my socks off, and you're gonna do it right."

He tugged her into the shoe boutique tucked into a storefront a few doors down from the dress shop. "My lady needs a pair of shoes," he said to the girl approaching him. "Heels."

"Of course, Mr. Patterson." She smiled at them both. "Right this way."

"Silver if you got 'em," he said.

The girl led them across the store. Shoes rested on Plexiglas shelves tucked into wooden slats. Every color glistened beneath the spotlights like art on a gallery wall. Jewels winked and sequins sparkled.

Ty pointed to a pair of sky-high glittery silver stilettos on a shelf halfway up. "Those will do."

"Ty, no!" Nisa protested. She'd break her ankle trying to walk in them. "I can't wear those!"

"Why not?" he asked. "They're perfect."

"They're too high. I'll fall." She searched his face. "Please."

Panic shot through her with the thunder of Ty's racecar motor for a split second before his features softened.

"Okay," he said. "Lower heel."

She sagged with relief. "Thank you."

"Think nothing of it. Tonight's supposed to be special. You won't be able to enjoy it if you're injured." He leaned so close that his lips caressed her ear. "But you would've looked so hot in those shoes."

Nisa shivered, at a loss for words as they headed for the pumps. The salesgirl pointed out a pair of cork wedges. Nisa shook her head, looking around the store. Her gaze lit on a pair of silver strappy sandals with a chunky two-inch heel. "Those sandals are pretty."

The girl asked about her size and disappeared into the back. Ty wandered the boutique looking at the other available accessories. Nisa watched as he picked out a silver beaded handbag barely large enough to carry a coin purse, cell phone and a tube of lipstick.

"Here you are." The store girl set the box on the bench seat and lifted the lid.

Nisa sat down and tried on the shoes. They fit perfectly. She walked up and down the aisle a couple times, checking for comfort.

"Beautiful."

Nisa stumbled. Ty was there in an instant, his hand steady on her elbow. "Easy, darlin'."

"I told you I couldn't do the stilettos." She flashed a cheeky grin.

"Point taken." He chuckled. "We'll take the pocketbook, too."

"Of course, Mr. Patterson." The salesgirl smiled. "Anything else?"

Is she flirting with my man under my nose? Nisa put the shoes back into the box and slipped back into her flats.

"How about a pair of earrings to go with the bag?" she persisted. "I have some beautiful silver and crystal chandeliers that would go great with those shoes."

Nisa shook her head. "I brought some with me."

Ty passed his credit card again, signing the slip with a flourish, then ushered Nisa back outside. "Was it me," he asked, "or was she way too pushy?"

"No, she was pushy." Nisa grimaced. "I'm pretty sure she was flirting with you, too."

Ty laughed. "Jealous, sweetheart?"

"Nope." She grinned. "You've told me you love me."

"Yes, I do." He rested his hands on her hips.

Her heart raced as his lips descended to hers. The first brush of his mouth erased thoughts of anyone else from her mind. When his tongue plundered, her knees threatened to buckle.

Ty broke away first. "Let's get ready for dinner. I can't wait to see you all dressed up."

Nisa was still dazed as Ty guided her back to the car. He stowed the purchases in the backseat and slid behind the wheel. As soon as she secured her seatbelt, he took off like a rocket back to his place.

Chapter 14

The butterflies returned with a vengeance as Nisa showered and changed into her dress. The crimson silk skimmed her curves in a whisper-light brush over the sexiest bra and panty set she owned, exciting her.

She slipped her feet into the silver sandals and fastened a pair of diamond studs into her lobes, then examined her reflection in the full-length mirror. Her neutral makeup made her eyes look larger and more luminous. She swiped a mocha-tinted stick across her lips and put the tube into her tiny purse.

"This is it," she told the stranger staring back at her. "Showtime."

Slightly stumbling in her heels, Nisa headed for the living room, the carpet muffling her footsteps. Ty stood at the window in the living room. He had one hand in his trousers pocket and held a tumbler of clear liquid in the other. He brought his arm up, tipping his head back as he took a drink.

She studied him for a moment, his face clear in the glass. Their gazes locked. His shoulders tensed as he turned around.

She held her breath, waiting for his reaction.

Ty set his glass on the coffee table as he strode to where she stood. His azure gaze was alight with desire. Heat pooled low in her abdomen and her pulse roared in her ears as he threaded his fingers through her hair.

"Mind blown." He brought her lips to his.

Her lashes fluttered closed as his mouth moved over hers, sweet from the soft drink he'd just consumed. Nisa whimpered in the back of her throat. Ty deepened the kiss, his tongue plundering hers. Her knees threatened to buckle as her bones melted in his heat.

At long last he broke the contact. "We'd better go."

Her breath heaved from her lungs in ragged gasps as they headed for his car. He opened the door for her and she slid into the seat, careful to not catch the hem of her gown on her sandals, and watched as he rounded the nose of the car and climbed in behind the wheel.

"I'm sorry." He started the car and headed down the driveway. "I didn't mean to smudge your lipstick."

"No worries." Nisa reapplied the color using the mirror on the back of her visor. "Where are we going?"

"You'll see." Ty drove further north, away from Charlotte along the shores of Lake Norman. He took her hand in his over the shifter and squeezed.

Reassurance and love flowed between them like a river, and she reveled in the emotions.

Ten minutes later they pulled into the parking lot of the restaurant and Ty killed the motor. "Thank you for coming with me tonight." He brushed his lips over the back of her hand.

"In case I forget to say it later, thank you." She smiled. "I had a great time."

"I hope you do, and that this is the first of many wonderful nights together."

Ty's words sent a shiver of delight and anticipation down Nisa's spine as they exited the car. He offered her his arm, and she wrapped her hand around his elbow as he escorted her into the restaurant. The hostess guided them to a table near the windows. The lake beyond glistened in twilight, the sun cascading ripples of gold across the still water as Ty pushed in Nisa's chair before taking his own opposite her. A few minutes later they had drinks, but Ty held off on ordering from the menu.

Nisa sipped her water. "Why did Cole ask me to fly down here if he wasn't going to say hi to me?"

"He asked you to come here for me." Ty took a drink from his glass. "Because I wanted …" He trailed off.

Nisa tensed, waiting for him to continue.

He shook his head, like he was trying to get his thoughts together. "Nisa, would you consider moving back to Charlotte?" he asked instead.

She sat back in her chair, confused. "Not in my present situation, no."

"What would it take?"

She eyed him warily. "Ty, what are you trying to say?"

He cleared his throat, his nervousness palpable. "That I want you with me always."

Nisa pondered his words, the air current swirling between them heavy with ... something. Anticipation? Attraction? Yes, both of those, but something else she couldn't identify.

When the waitress asked if they were ready to order, Ty waved her away.

Taking advantage of the delay, Nisa excused herself to use the ladies' room. She gripped the counter in the ladies' lounge, energy zinging across her nerves as she stared at her reflection. Her eyes were dreamy and a little unfocused, and her mouth looked thoroughly kissed. Which she had been, she thought with a slight twist of her lips.

She reapplied her lipstick though she didn't need it, and wiped a smudge of mascara from beneath her left eye.

Splashing cold water onto her wrists, she tried calming her racing heart. After drying her hands, she headed back to the table. Halfway across the room she gasped, stopping dead in her tracks. *What the –?*

Nisa forced her legs to move and she strode to her seat. "What are you doing here?" she asked her brother. Her knees gave out as she half-sat, half-tumbled into her chair.

"Ty asked me to join you." Cole stood and hugged her.

Her thoughts tornadoed through her brain. "But you two usually avoid each other like the plague. Why would you risk scandal, being seen together in public?"

"It seems we have something in common now." Cole's lips twisted into a wry smile. "You."

Confused by the strange behavior of these two infuriating, handsome men, she frowned. "I – I don't –"

Ty tenderly took her hand in his. "Nisa, I've never met anyone like you. You're amazing, smart and beautiful. I love you so much, and I can't imagine the rest of my life without you." His thumb stroked her knuckles. "I realize we need to work out some major issues, but I know we can overcome them together."

"I love you too, Ty, but –" she broke off, unsure of how to finish her sentence.

Ty's eyes shimmered as his grasp tightened on her fingers. "I'm making a mess of this." He shook his head. "What I'm trying to say is, Nisa, will you marry me?"

She gasped in surprise. "I – I wasn't expec –" Tears pricked her eyes, but she blinked them away. She glanced at her brother, whose broad smile encouraged her. Joy and love scrambled her thoughts into a twisted jumble. "Yes! Oh my gosh, yes, I will."

Ty rounded the table and kissed Nisa, lifting her completely from her seat when he wrapped her in his arms.

"I can't tell you how happy you've made me," he said. "I love you so much."

"I love you too." She returned his kisses with equal fervor.

Ty was the first to break away as he set her back on her feet. Taking her left hand in his, he slid a brilliant diamond ring onto her finger. He pressed a kiss over the ring, then her lips.

Cole stood and shook hands with his competitor, then he hugged Nisa tight. "I'm so happy for you, sis. Congratulations."

"Wait." Nisa leaned back so she could look into her brother's hazel-green eyes. Their father's eyes. "You knew?"

"Of course, I did." Cole chuckled. "How else would I have gotten you here?"

"You made it sound …" she trailed off, realization dawning.

"I thought my baby sister getting engaged was important." He hugged her again. "I know how you feel about being back here, but I'm glad you're willing to try."

Nisa couldn't breathe. She stared at the gorgeous ring, recognizing the design instantly from her Love's Kiss collection, the diamond flanked by glowing sapphires set in white gold. One thought stood out among the others swirling through her mind. "My collection hasn't launched yet. How did you get one made so fast?"

Ty gave her a sheepish grin. "Viktor helped."

Nisa nodded. Of course he had. So many emotions swamped her, and she couldn't control them. Especially since the chances were high that she'd end up moving back to the city that took almost everything away from her, to be with a man who shared her father's passion.

It made the most sense, though. His job was here, and she had no doubt she could design jewelry anywhere.

Even for Viktor. Her pulse pounded in her ears and her vision dimmed. For a moment she felt faint, but she was able to stay upright.

"Hey, are you okay?" Ty brushed his knuckles along her cheek.

Shaking off her jumbled thoughts, Nisa gave him a tremulous smile. "It's a lot to take in," she admitted candidly. "I wasn't expecting a proposal."

They both sat down, and Ty took her hand across the table.

"Ty and I talked." Cole broke the awkward silence. "He asked for my blessing."

"I know how you feel about racing," Ty added earnestly. "What it took from you."

Nisa inhaled sharply at the reminder, but said nothing as he continued.

"But I want to give something back." His gaze captured hers.

She couldn't look away, and the intensity of the blazing emotions robbed her of the ability to speak.

"How can I say this without sounding like a selfish jackass?" Ty said aloud, as if trying to gather his thoughts. "I want to give you a family. My family. The one at the racetrack and the one I grew up with."

The air evaporated in her lungs. It had been just her and Cole for so long. "I –" She broke off. Her thoughts knotted in her head and she found it impossible to form a coherent sentence.

"Wow, sis." Cole chuckled. "I don't think I've ever seen you speechless."

The jibe shook her from her jumbled emotions. "I'm glad you find it amusing," she said, her tone lightly derisive as she glanced at Ty.

He wasn't smiling. In fact, his face paled into a weird greenish color beneath his perpetual tan.

Oh, God. I'm the one who's selfish! The thought jolted her back to the present. "Ty." She reached for his hand. "I have to tell you something. I had coffee with an old classmate a few weeks ago, and he made me realize something."

He tensed beneath her touch but didn't interrupt, for which she was grateful. If he had, she'd probably have lost her nerve. "He made me realize that I'm still Nisa Forester, the daughter of Gary and the sister of Cole and Angela, even after I left Charlotte all those years ago."

She reached for her water glass, but her hand shook and she nearly knocked it over. "He got me thinking. Of everything I don't have in my life, but also of everything I do have. Most importantly, I have the love of a good man. I'd be foolish to throw that away."

Flame ignited in his gaze. "Does that mean what I think it means?"

The last few moments made her realize that, even though she moved to Wisconsin as a child, her heart had never really left the Carolinas. He was right; they did have some issues, but they would work them out together.

"It means I'll be moving back to Charlotte." Her lips twitched into a small smile as a huge weight lifted from her chest. Now that the decision had been made, she wouldn't renege. "It wouldn't make sense for you to move to Wisconsin when your work is here."

He twined his fingers with hers. "I can't tell you how much that means to me."

The waitress chose that moment to stop by, and Nisa's stomach growled at the reminder as Ty released her hand. With her seesawing emotions she hadn't given food a thought since they'd entered the restaurant, but she was suddenly ravenous. She glanced at the menu and placed her order, then lifted her water glass with a hand that was steadier than it had been minutes ago. Taking a sip, she glanced out the window.

The sun disappeared behind the mountains, but fingers of pink and orange light speared the inky sky like beacons of hope in a bleak world. A smothering weight crushed her chest, like she was being wrapped in a hug, and she fought to fill her lungs with air. She snuck a covert glance at her brother, who was talking with Ty and the waitress as he, too, placed his order. Neither was paying attention to her as she took a few moments to regain her equilibrium.

A second later the pressure eased as an immense peace flowed through her, and she *felt* her father's love pour into her heart so strongly that it brought tears to her eyes. *I love you too, Daddy.* The weight dissipated, as did her fears about Ty and his career.

Nisa turned back to the two most wonderful men she'd ever met and smiled. The dark cloud of her past lifted, and she couldn't wait to start a much brighter future.

About the Author

Reading and writing have always been a part of CJ's life. Ever since she can remember, she's been putting pen to paper, creating complex characters in rich environments. She lives in Western Wisconsin with her husband and fur-baby.

When she's not working or writing, she enjoys baking, cake decorating, and of course, watching NASCAR. She picked up her first piping bag at age fourteen and started decorating full-time at age twenty-three. Using the experience she'd gained while working in her family's bakery, along with her love of racing, she created the setting for her first series of novels.

Follow her on social media and her website. She loves to hear from her readers.

cjbowerauthor@hotmail.com
www.cjbowerauthor.wordpress.com
www.facebook.com/CJBowerAuthor

Additional Reading by CJ Bower

On Track with Icing: Caked with Pleasure book 1

She's everything he wanted in a woman…except for one thing.

Plus-sized bakery owner Jacqui Jacobson's confidence is at an all-time low after her public divorce and her ex-husband's despicable accusations. So the last person she expects to show interest in her is racing hot-shot Nick Barrister. But when the two click over her risqué cake designs, it seems like icing on the cake.

However, Jacqui hasn't told him that not being able to have children was the main cause for her marriage ending. As her relationship with Nick turns from casual to serious he expresses his desire for children, and now time is running out. Can she tell him first before her ex-husband, who has reared his ugly head and is determined to destroy her new-found happiness, beats her to it? And will Nick still want her once he finds out?

Content Warning: contains lots of steamy sexual content and exciting racing action

Icing the Competition: Caked with Pleasure book 2

Can the innocent beauty heal the arrogant stock car driver's heart?

Shawn Sheldon comes home early from Daytona and discovers his wife Lisa in their bed with two men. He immediately kicks her out and files for divorce, but the hits keep blindsiding him like a high-speed crash at Talladega. Shattered by Lisa's betrayal, Shawn takes a self-imposed sabbatical to let his heart heal. However, a chance encounter with the beautiful Persephone encourages him to try again.

Persephone Williams has harbored a secret crush on Shawn since their introduction a year ago. While she's dated in the past, she's never had a steady boyfriend, and none of them inspired her to punch her V-card. After one hot, steamy kiss with Shawn, she finds herself giving in to the desires of her heart. He is arrogant—cocky, even—but he proves that he has a soft side too.

When Shawn's ex-wife resurfaces and tries digging her red-lacquered talons into him again, he shows Peri that she's the one he wants. But can Peri handle his high-profile career and the media circus that goes with it?

Content Warning: contains steamy sex and hot racing action

Love in Victory Lane: In It to Win It anthology

Racing is all Catalina Bryant ever wanted to do. She's spent the past fifteen years climbing the ranks and paying her dues, which included fighting off slurs and innuendoes regarding her gender. Overcoming many setbacks, she has finally made it to the highest level in NASCAR and is on the eve of starting her rookie season.

Her new crew chief, Chad Kiesgen, is incredible. He has a strong work ethic and amazing integrity. Just the guy to help her achieve her goal. However, she hits a speed bump when the sizzling chemistry between them carries over to their personal lives, which could damage both of their careers.

But another man lurks in the background wanting Cat for himself, and will stop at nothing to claim her. Will Cat find love in Victory Lane, or will her career crash and burn before she leaves the starting line?

Content Warning: all six stories contain steamy sex scenes. My story contains hot racing action. Others contain adult language.